A White Angel

Also by Peter Pennington

William Wood's Diary

A WHITE ANGEL

Peter Pennington

Ardnamona Publishers
Stansted, MMXV

First published in the UK by
Ardnamona Publishers

ISBN 978-0-9542057-1-3

Typeset in Garamond by Ian Kegel
Printed by Catford Print Centre, London

ARDNAMONA PUBLISHERS
22 Brewery Lane
Stansted, Essex CM24 8LB UK

www.ardnamonapublishers.co.uk

DEDICATION

In a story that traces the history of a family through so many historical events of tragedy and war, it is only right to dedicate the book to those in the medical and nursing professions who in turn dedicate themselves to alleviating the suffering of others. As a child I was brought up in a medical household, and where "the patient always came first".

This book would never have been completed but for the skills and care shown to me personally by the doctors and nurses at the Cambridge University Addenbrooke's Hospital in England.

So to them and all their professional colleagues past and present world-wide this book is dedicated with deep thanks.

CONTENTS

LIST OF ILLUSTRATIONS

FOREWORD

September 11th was one of those wonderful clear Fall mornings, blue skies, ne'er a cloud and obviously the temps were going to rise to mid 70s. As I walked by the East River to my office on the Upper East Side, I thought I was lucky to be working in such a city.

I arrived at the independent girls school where I was Head and watched the girls coming to school so full of life and fun and I was filled with happiness also. I went to my first meeting in my office, and was mulling over some problem with my Board Chair, when my assistant put her head around the door and said she thought we should know that a plane had crashed into one of the towers of the World Trade Center. We were upset, but of course thought it was an accident. It wasn't until she came back some minutes later and told us that a second plane had hit the other tower and parents were calling that I jumped into action; finally realizing that something was very wrong. Then started a day of worry and concern. How many of the girls had parents working in the Towers? How many families would be affected? How would we care for the girls who would not be able to get home once the bridges had been closed? How to keep everyone calm?

By this time clouds of smoke were rising from the towers and it reminded me of growing up on the outskirts of Liverpool in England when the city was being blitzed. Perhaps that experience helped because I could tell the school, that terrible though it was, they would probably be OK and life would return to normal. We carried on with school classes and tried to make the day as normal as possible, which I think the girls appreciated. Many parents came to pick their children up throughout the day, others could not get there until late. As a community we were comparatively lucky, losing no present parents, but we had our tragedies, loss of alumnae, a faculty spouse, uncles on the planes.

Peter Pennington has depicted the day well in his most interesting biography of an immigrant family. He grew up in the same area as I did so experienced World War II in Liverpool also. He has been wanting to write this book for a long time, but wanted to wait until a fictional account of September 11th would be acceptable to people. That time has arrived!

Priscilla M Winn Barlow
Head of School

PREFACE

Many nations and many religions claim to have special days in their histories and which they believe changed their lives and those of their fellow countrymen and women or their co-believers. Yet very few of these events can be said to have had an impact on the lives of virtually everyone in the world.

In modern history – and certainly so far for the twenty-first century – the happenings in New York's Manhattan on September 11th 2001 have been unique in that respect. They were to change the way most of us go about our daily lives, the way we look at our fellow human beings, and how we and the society around us all interact with each other.

In writing a book about such an event one is inevitably going to find others who disagree on the selection of subjects and the interpretation of facts. I leave that field of argument to future professional historians.

There will be others who will question the right of an Englishman to intrude on some very private moments of the modern American way of life, but I hope that others will agree that perhaps an outsider can bring a sense of balance and history to such a traumatic happening. By keeping the story in a fictional form and linking it to earlier times I have tried to pay tribute to the sheer courage, and what in England we would call "guts", of New Yorkers in facing up to the tragedy that was "9/11".

All of us of whatever race and colour are shaped and moulded by our family backgrounds and history. I have selected one fictional family from a background of the type of which I am familiar. It is only one of many but I hope it provides an entertaining read as well as a serious tribute.

When writing this book I have received so much help from so many friends, family and complete strangers that I cannot name them all. One group, some of whom are old school friends from over sixty years ago and now scattered across the globe, volunteered to read it chapter by chapter and tell me where I was going wrong. I cannot thank them enough. Others have helped me with modern technology to go down the route of self-publishing and print-on-demand and which is so different to my earlier efforts. They have all been incredible with their support, as have my immediate family whose tolerances humble me.

I need only one word in contemporary English to say to you the reader: "Enjoy!"

Peter Pennington
Stansted, England
February 2015

ACKNOWLEDGEMENTS

Tullio Ferro, Desenzano
The late Hugh Fetherstonhaugh, Montreal
The late Flora Kidd, New Brunswick
The late Jay Underwood, Nova Scotia
Beryl & Derek Alker
Hilde Coppus
Sam Donabie
Reg & Eileen Jones
Brenda Kegel
Gillian Kegel
Ian Kegel
James Pennington
Mary & David Willans
Priscilla Winn Barlow
Hotel Piccola Vela, Desenzano
Biblioteca di Desenzano del Garda
New York Municipal Archives
New York Public Library, Map Division
University Library, Cambridge, England
and others...

MAPS

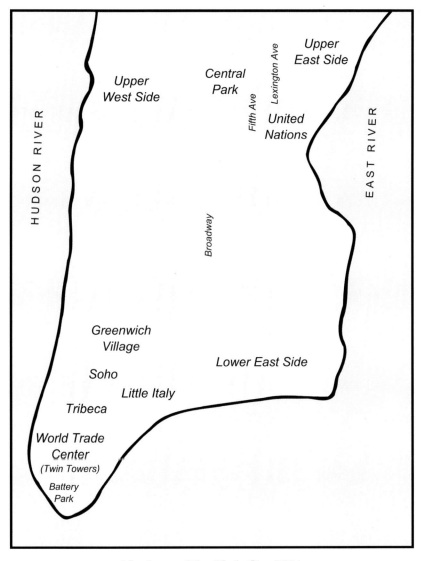

Manhattan, New York City, 2001

Great Britain and Ireland

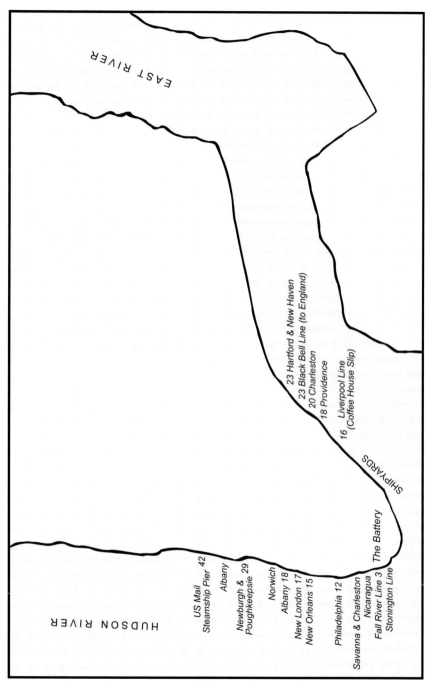

Lower Manhattan circa 1855, showing coastal steamer piers

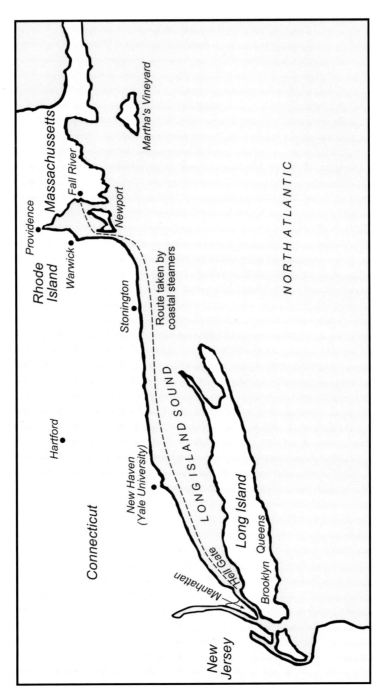

Long Island Sound showing the routes of coastal steamers, mid to late 19ᵗʰ century

Eastern Canada, showing the route of the Intercolonial Railway

Italy

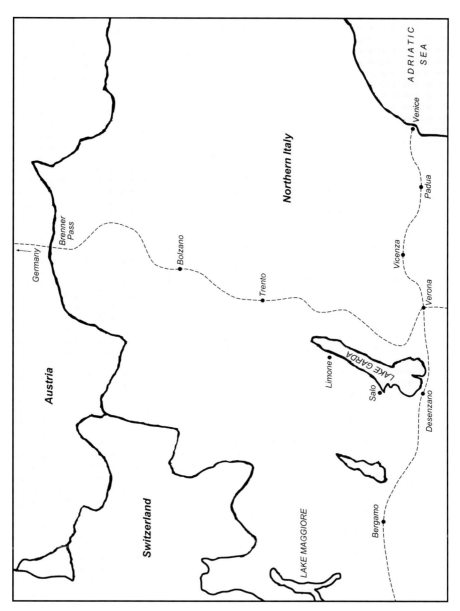

Lake Garda and Northern Italy showing the main railway routes

THE JACKSON FAMILY TREE

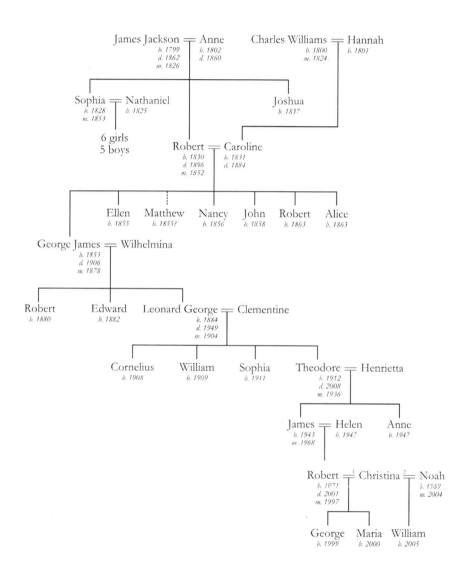

A White Angel

CHAPTER I

The South Tower, September 11th 2001

The elevator was not quite so full as usual for the start of the day as it rapidly rose through the floors of the South Tower of the World Trade Center.

A few minutes before, as he had walked to the building amongst the normal hurly-burly of the Manhattan rush-hour, Robert had thought to himself what a beautiful morning it was. One of those clear and warm September days that served for all New Yorkers as a final glow of comfort before the onslaught of winter.

The bright blue sky with the sun streaming in over the East River had beckoned him out of bed that morning. He had stood by the window, and stretched out his limbs in tribute to the sun. As he had done so he had gazed down at Christina, his partner, lover and wife for the last four years. She had half-murmured as she turned over in response to his usual early departure from their bed; but her eyes were still closed as he bent down and gently pressed his lips to hers in adoration of that beautiful creature who lay there. From somewhere in the sheets there came a satisfying gurgle of delight, a momentary flicker of half-open eyes and she returned to her world of dreams with the comforting feeling that there were many more such mornings to come over the years ahead.

Life, married life, and especially here in the affluent Upper East Side of New York City, was well worth enduring despite the hassle, the traffic, the crowded subways and even the heat of summer when all sensible folk departed and the north-south running "avenues" and east-west "streets" were taken over by tourists from all parts of the globe.

But today, September 11ᵗʰ 2001, was one of those wonderful New York days when the tourists had mostly departed; the air was still warm and New York once again belonged to New Yorkers. It was a day to savour, an ordinary working day to be spent in the most wonderful city in the world; and when all was at peace with the world.

Nobody in all of that great city – from the doorman downstairs, who tipped his hat and said 'Good morning, Mr Robert. Have a nice day' when he later left for the office – to Mayor Giuliani himself whose official residence was only a stone's throw from where Robert and Christina lived – knew that that morning was maybe the last the world would ever know when it would be at peace with itself.

Last night however had not been all that peaceful back in the apartment. As Robert emerged from the subway and made his way along to the office he started to think about their two year old, little George. Something had been bothering the child. Maybe it was a new tooth coming through, but whatever it was he had taken hours to go to sleep. That suspected tooth had given the little one earache and it had been ages before Robert and Christina had had one of those nights together that was destined to be remembered by one of them for a long long time to come.

As the doors of the elevator in the South Tower moved aside Robert knew instinctively that he had reached his floor and without glancing upwards he headed straight for the water-cooler, helped himself to a cup and then carefully threaded his way through the network of desks to his own by the window.

He was lucky to have that view over towards Staten Island and the Verrazano Narrows Bridge in the distance. But then he had a good job as a trader.

Most days he spent much of his time talking to his opposite number in London England and only just before the school vacation he had been over there for four days. London was a good city to visit and all his trips seemed to be non-stop with breakfast meetings followed by long days. Each evening one or another of his colleagues insisted on "showing him the town".

Those nights in London always started, and sometimes finished, in a pub. There was something very special about that very British institution, "the pub". Even the warm beer was worth putting up with, if one could soak-in the cheerful friendliness that came from all around as they stood at the bar. Each of the "locals", as the regular patrons were called, seemed to have their own favourite way of drinking the beer. Some used a straight-sided glass, others a round glass with a handle and yet others insisted on a pewter tankard that seemed to be kept specially for them on their very own hook on the ancient beams that supported the ceiling.

Everyone knew everyone and any visitor from New York was always welcomed. He had been told time and time again how this one or that one had recently been there, done a show and strolled through Central Park or taken the free ferry over to Staten Island to get the view back to Manhattan. When Robert had said he worked in one of those two tall towers he had often been greeted with comments such as 'you lucky fella, what a wonderful view you must have'.

And yes Robert did consider himself lucky to have that view. As he sat down at his desk that morning he thought back to those recent London nights. Nights that had once or twice finished with yet more beers at 4am in a pub called the "Red Rose" somewhere near Covent Garden. "Lucky fella" – a funny, yet somehow typically English, term.

He could never live in London, for all its friendliness towards foreign visitors. He had detected another side to England and its way of life that was not for him. Amongst themselves the Brits were "stuffy". There was a lingering reserve that seemed to come from a general acceptance of class-distinction. No one would admit to it, yet everyone appeared to subconsciously accept their own "place" in the structure of it. It was so much at odds with the freedoms and equality that he knew in New York and which were part of the American way of life. In Manhattan no one was "inferior" or "superior" because they had a certain parent or lived in a particular district. Sure people were different in degrees of wealth but it was up to each and everyone to aspire to, and to work towards getting to, the top of the pile. That was the American Way and of course it was a better way. He, Robert, had worked hard and still did as a trader, and his reward was a beautiful wife, two lovely children and a fine apartment. He suspected the difference between the two ways of life, the restrictive backward British approach and the freedom-loving and open attitude of the New Yorkers, was to be found as much in the home as in the boardroom, or even around the office water-cooler.

There was another difference between those two big cities. In a sense it was rather like the difference between the two Twin Towers. Outwardly they were the same but within their walls those who knew them well were aware of differences of character and even of each having its separate soul. New York City liked to think of itself as the centre of the world and in terms of modern day power and influence none could deny this was the case. London by contrast was in a way more cosmopolitan. In New York there was a big range of folk of all colours and creeds. There was a mixture of languages to be heard on the Subway; English of course but also Spanish and a host of other indecipherable tongues that one suspected could be Polish or Greek or even Arabic, yet many of them had an American tinge to the pronunciation. And almost everyone was an American.

Sure there were some in the Tower who came from other countries but they were working short-term in Manhattan and would eventually go back to their own countries. Within his own company, and on this very floor, there were certainly Hispanics and African-Americans, all part of the rich mixture of races that made up their country. Moreover there was no deference for gender in the American workplace. He sometimes secretly admired the ravishingly good looks of some of the African-American women and who seemed to cultivate an air of mysticism about them that intrigued Robert.

By contrast in those London offices there was that half-hidden society pyramid. The fair sex was more common now at the higher echelons of the company offices over there than had been the case when he first had visited the city. However Hispanics, and the Brits' equivalent of African-Americans, were seldom to be found. Fewer of the women at their desks seemed to have the same sophistication of self-assurance and gender equality than was to be found back in the US.

In a way London was more broad in its range of faces and languages. As you travelled on the "Tube", as they called the Subway, you could see and hear folk from so many lands. It seemed to Robert that, in England if you were at the bottom of the pyramid, there was a greater chance of having a darker skin and of speaking a language other than English. Yet paradoxically many of these people from all over the world, and whatever their skin or race, considered themselves "at home" in England. England seemed to be considered by so many "home" whether you were born in Australia, India, Zimbabwe or Jamaica. Funny people these English – very funny.

Anyway they, Robert, Christina, little George and baby Maria owed their allegiance to the Stars and Stripes and like all Americans they were proud of their country. It was good to be an American at eight o'clock on that beautiful morning of September 11th 2001.

After their marriage in 1997 Robert had taken Christina for a trip to Europe and they had spent a week in London. They had gone to a different theatre every evening and he had shown her all the sights, including Big Ben and Buckingham Palace where they had watched the "Changing of the Guard" on a sultry hot day. They had wondered how the soldiers managed to survive underneath those big black "bearskin" hats and which really were made from the pelts of black bears. One day they had visited London's own Tower – "The Tower of London" and which was many hundreds of years older than the South Tower where he had the privilege of working in New York. They had walked in St James' Park and shopped in Oxford Street; but Christina had not found the shops as good as those back home. The fashions were much less sophisticated to her eyes and the window displays did not match those of Saks or Bloomingdales.

After London they had gone to Paris. They had not flown to Paris like most Americans but instead had been assured by their travel agent on Lexington Avenue back home when planning the trip, that it would be almost as quick, and would be a very special experience, to go from London to Paris by train through the Channel Tunnel. They had accepted her advice and made the two hour journey sitting in their "first class" (that again was something typically British, being described as a "first-class" passenger) train seats. Looking out of the windows as they left London they could see row upon row of small drab houses each with its chimney pots for their coal fires. Even the odd tree seemed to have a layer of ancient dirt and smoke hanging on every leaf. Then the countryside with its funny-looking tall bee-hive shaped buildings called "oast-houses" started to appear. They were used for turning the locally-grown hops into those warm British beers.

All of a sudden, after an announcement by the train controller, they had rushed into a tunnel that seemed to go on and on. They were deep under the sea. Under the "English Channel" (as the British called it, "La Manche" meaning "sleeve" as the French referred to it). Robert had read in his history books about The Channel and its place in English history. For the English it had always been a great defence object securing them from any potential invader from the other side.

The Romans had to cross this twenty mile stretch of open water in their first attempt to invade Britain more than fifty years before the birth of Christ. Then the Normans had come a thousand years later from France to conquer England and had set up a system of monarchy that existed to this very day. But the Normans in 1066 were the last to make a successful crossing and invade the country. Later the Spanish with their "Armada" of invasion ships, then the French soldiers of Napoleon and finally Hitler's Nazi armies had all found the English Channel a line of defence that had proved impenetrable to their political aims. For nine hundred years that twenty miles of water had said "thus far, no further" to invading armies. But now he and Christina were under the waves, sitting in those comfortable "first class" train seats and within 30 minutes were out again and racing away through the French countryside.

In Northern France the landscape was one of open rolling fields now all so beautiful and peaceful under the summer sun. They were peaceful today but twice earlier that century those same fields had reverberated to gun-fire as bombardment after bombardment had hurtled shells to and fro between opposing armies. Twice in a century those rolling wheat fields had been deeply scarred by muddy trenches full of dead and dying men. Those, now-pretty, villages had been reduced to rubble with sometimes only the local church left standing – and not even all those had been spared. The little copses of woods that now stood under the blazing summer sun had seen their trees stripped bare of every living sign of greenery. Yet Nature had re-asserted its influence and thankfully the French "paysage" had covered up its wounds.

Mankind had been less prepared to forgive and forget its own sufferings. Beside the train track every so often would appear war cemeteries. Sometimes French, sometimes British or Canadian or even German. Each nation looked after its own dead in its own fashion as they lay beneath that summer sun in neat rows, with crosses, Stars of David, plain white headstones or for the Germans metal crosses, to mark their individual contributions to history.

That day the small French towns with outwardly dull-looking grey-coloured churches, each with its spire, looked so peaceful from the train window. Robert had read, and he told Christina as they sped along at nearly 200 miles per hour, that each of those little towns had its own war memorial. Often simple edifices made of local stone, they listed the names not just of its brave soldiers who had died in the two world wars of the Twentieth Century, but also often the name of those who had fallen fighting the German invaders of 1870. Many had a fourth list. This was not of soldiers but of villagers, frequently old men and women, who had been put up against the walls of those same dull looking churches and "fusillé par les Allemands" ("shot by the Germans") when helping American and other allied airmen and soldiers to escape during the 1939-45 war. Christina had gazed deep into Robert's eyes and said quietly, 'Thank God we live in a time of peace and that you will never get involved in things like that.' He had leant across the train's table as the French countryside flashed past and had gently squeezed her hand.

All those sober thoughts and history-book memories had been put behind them when Robert and Christina were in Paris. They were a young newly-married couple and they were out for fun. The buildings were magnificent, the Opera was a great success and those shops... Christina especially liked the lingerie departments where she vanished off for a few minutes only to come back with a neatly wrapped little parcel of contents to show Robert after they came back from one of those risqué late-night shows up in Montmartre. Then they had flown on to Rome, Italy and seen the Holy Father giving his weekly blessing to the faithful from a window high above the square in front of the Vatican Palace. That was another of those funny things about Europe. The Vatican was not just a city, it was a separate country in the middle of the capital city of Italy.

It had been a wonderful honeymoon and one they knew they would both remember together far into their old age.

Now in 2001 they had moved to the next stage in life and instead of being "the children" to their parents they had their own offspring. They would have to start planning another trip to Europe as a family and take George and Maria with them. Buckingham Palace with its red uniformed guards, Paris with the Eiffel Tower to climb and the Colosseum in Rome to see. The children would be thrilled. Perhaps better to wait two or three years and then they would really appreciate those sights.

Robert pulled himself together. All this dreaming was fine but it was now nearly nine o'clock on a Tuesday morning and he must get on with his work.

It was already after lunch-time in London and his phone could start getting hot any minute with the latest trades. There were a couple of deals he wanted to put through that day as they were of particular value to the firm. He also had a trip to Frankfurt in Germany to put together as it must be made this fall.

Sure enough at that moment the phone rang. It was Ed – his opposite number at the office in Canary Wharf in London. Ed needed to talk over some prices of deals already done before Robert had kissed those sweet lips of Christina as he had left their apartment. Robert lent forward on the desk, one hand gripping the phone the other twirling his pencil and starting to scribble notes on a blank sheet of paper before him. The conversation started to flow across the three thousand miles of Atlantic Ocean that lay between them.

At that moment Robert half-glanced up and gazed out of the window. Something floated past his eyes without him fully taking it in. Perhaps one of his contact lenses was not in properly, or his eyes were out of focus for a split second. It had almost seemed as if a plane had crossed his line of vision but that was ridiculous. Yet the next moment he heard a muffled bang and he broke off his conversation with Ed back in London. All of a sudden he could see that there was smoke billowing out of the building opposite. Something had hit the "twin". Rachel, the African-American with the long legs that were always best displayed when she wore her mini-skirts in summer, had gotten up from her desk and was at his side staring out of the window.

'Jesus,' was all Robert could say. 'Jesus, some damn fool of a pilot has come down too low and hit the other tower. Ed, call me back, something has happened,' he managed to choke into the London phone.

Beside him Rachel was starting to shake as they both witnessed the plumes of smoke beginning to pour out from the North Tower. Without thinking he automatically put his arm round Rachel's shoulder. It was the most natural thing. The girl needed comforting although he himself was feeling a few tremors starting to run through his own body.

'My God, just look at that,' she whispered.

The fire seemed to be spreading right across the building. Then a thought started to creep across his mind.

'However are those poor guys on the upper floors going to get out?' he spluttered to Rachel.

The phone rang on his desk and without thinking he picked it up. It was Ed again in London.

'What the hell is going on there?' the voice carried down the line. 'We were talking to Henry Lee in the other building and the line has gone dead. Is something wrong?'

Christina and Robert had lived on East 76th Street ever since they had got back from that wonderful first visit to Europe. They were fortunate. They had money thanks to all the hard work Robert was putting in and a friend of his father's had managed to use his influence to get them approved by the other residents so that they could start off married life in a comfortable fashion. Every morning he was in town Robert took the subway from 77th Street to Fulton Street and then walked to the office. He had done so this morning.

That morning no sooner had Robert left for work than Christina was herself up and about. She showered and got the children out of their beds and dressed them. Rosa – who came to help her with the apartment and the children each day – arrived early; perhaps the beautiful morning had inspired her also to start work, even before time. Christina left the children with her and walked to the bagel shop around the corner on York Avenue. She and Rosa would have them before she took the children for a walk in Central Park. It was such a fine day, not a cloud in the sky and there would be plenty of mothers with their push-chairs and toddlers in the park. There were always birds to watch as they pecked on the ground and the odd squirrel would rush up into the branches to the delight of the watching children. This was fall at its best, not just any fall, but a New York fall at its finest. They were lucky to be Americans – and lucky to live at this time and in this wonderful city.

Christina returned from the shop, placed the bagels on the slab in the kitchen and went to her room to look out a pair of shoes she would need for dinner that evening. Suddenly there was a rapid hammering on the door and at the same time the bell rang with an imperious demand rather than in its normal dulcet tone. Not the usual short brief couple of rings but a continual, urgent, demand for the front door to be opened.

She decided to answer the call herself. Obviously someone was in trouble and needed help; but she was beaten to the handle by Rosa who had quickly put down the vacuum cleaner that she had been using and had strode over to the panelled entrance to the apartment. As the door opened it was to reveal a distraught figure half-covered in a white bath-robe and topped with languid damp dark hair that had obviously left the shower behind only moments before. It took Christina a few seconds to recognise the black and white apparition that stood before her. It was Elena her neighbour from number 3C on the same floor.

They often said 'Hi' when they met in the elevator, but were not buddies by any stretch of the imagination. Elena's husband Tom and Robert did sometimes go into town together on the subway if they happened to meet in the elevator. They had originally met one day whilst out running and had discovered that they went to the same gym and worked near each other in the opposite towers. Sure they had something in common but they had never developed a close relationship, no more than had their respective wives. Christina remembered that Robert had said one day that he had done a deal with Tom and his firm and that since then several million dollars had flowed between the two companies.

As she stood there damp and half-naked Elena could scarcely get any words out. She had just left the shower after twenty minutes of warm cleansing water had been allowed to course over her beautiful body. She always looked forward to those hours with the sun streaming in over the East River and when even the Avenue below the block was still fairly quiet. That Tuesday morning was such a day and Elena had stayed in bed after Tom had left for the office. A gentle doze followed by a long refreshing shower and then she intended a trip downtown to do some shopping.

Elena had stepped out of the shower and gone into the bedroom where the TV was on, but the voices seemed somehow different to-day. They appeared to be screaming for attention and she heard the words 'World Trade Center' and 'Twin Towers' kept on popping up. Then there was something about a plane. Suddenly like a flash her mind became concentrated. That was Tom's building. Her Tom's building, the one to which he had left to go only a short while ago. All of a sudden Elena needed company, and quickly. Christina, next door, was the obvious first choice.

As soon as Elena managed to get something out it only took a moment for Christina to put her TV on. They could see the North Tower where Tom worked and even as they watched the plumes of grey smoke seemed to billow upwards by the minute. Elena began to sob and Christina put her arms round her.

'Don't worry,' she heard herself say as she tried to comfort her distressed neighbour. 'They have rehearsals for this sort of thing, and anyway it must have been a small plane.'

Five miles away Robert was also staring at the growing pall of smoke opposite. His arm was round Rachel's waist and she was beginning to weep.

'Those poor bastards,' she murmured as Robert ran the fingers of his other hand gently through her black hair that finished in a knot above the nape of her neck.

There was a general hush in the office as people stood in small groups watching the developing tragedy in their nearby sister building. The eerie silence was brusquely broken by someone's cell phone at the far end.

'What, oh my God!' came floating down the room as a trader who had only recently arrived from Georgia started to talk in an ever more highly-pitched voice.

'Say that again! Say that again!'

He started to scream into the mouthpiece. Then turning to a small stoutish woman who had flown in that morning from Chicago he said in a suddenly very sombre tone that was heard by all in the otherwise silent office.

'That was Jake over in the other tower. He says the lifts are not working and they can't get down the stairs because of the smoke.'

'Look!' yelled someone. 'A guy has fallen out of a window!'

'Not fallen,' came a response from another. 'The poor fellow jumped. I saw him do it.'

By now the quiet in the room had been penetrated by enough high tension to run a power station. All of a sudden it broke.

'Let's get the hell outta here,' came from a Texan drawl.

There was a general move towards the exit.

'Come on!' said Robert as he grabbed Rachel's elbow. 'Let's move.'

Pausing only to pick up her lipstick Rachel found herself being propelled toward the stairs. People from the floors above were of the same mind and it seemed that hundreds, if not thousands, were on their way out of the building. There was no panic rush, the numbers were too great for that. Just a hurried, orderly and determined march downwards towards the floors below and the exit. Some were carrying their briefcases, some had picked up family photographs from their desks. There were men with their sleeves rolled up just as they had prepared to start the day's work, women still with their coats on. One woman who had been trapped in the melee to reach her door onto the stairs had a bleeding nose.

At that moment the whole building shuddered and everyone about Robert and Rachel halted.

'Go back up!' a voice from below shouted urgently. 'There's no way down here.'

The previous orderly tide of hurried marchers going downwards turned into a flight upwards. Women were beginning to scream, the elderly were starting to pant with exhaustion and one man was pausing, holding onto the side of the wall, his face grey, with fear starting to stare out of his eyes. The woman with the bleeding nose was beginning to cry. Out of the corner of his eye Robert could see that Rachel's jaw had dropped and her fingers were now closely entwined in his as they breathlessly retraced their steps upwards.

Finally reaching their own floor it was to find the place empty. No one else had come back into their office, for all had continued the ever- upwards ascent on the stairs. By now Rachel was weeping copiously. Robert sat her gently down and went over to the water fountain to bring her a cup to sip. He was worried, worried like hell, but he was determined not to show it. His cellphone rang. It was an almost-screaming Christina.

'Where the hell are you? Are you OK?' She was bordering on the hysterical.

'I'm OK honey,' he replied. 'Not sure what's happened.'

'A plane, no two planes,' came the response. 'One hit each tower. Elena is with me, she cannot contact Tom.'

'Call you back, love you,' he replied trying to sound as matter-of-fact as he could.

By now they could scarcely see out of the window for smoke. Something flashed past the window.

'Christ!' Rachel said. 'That was a man.'

Slowly at first but then with an ever growing sense of ghastly realisation each of them began to wonder if this was the end. Was there to be no way out?

Below them flames and smoke blocked their escape. Above them others had decided that their only slim chance was to jump. Rachel had stopped sobbing now. She was pressing very close to Robert. He could feel her thumping heart through her flimsy blouse.

'This, is it, the end?' she whispered. 'Is it?'

'I think so,' he half replied, unable to believe he was uttering the words.

At that moment there was a loud crack and the whole building seemed to shudder. One minute Rachel was there, then there was nothing. No Rachel, no office, not even a floor. Just a choking dust and space. Space all around and nothingness. A tightening in his chest, stars before his eyes. Robert, husband of Christina, father of George and Maria, passed into history.

Christina and Elena gazed with horror, unbelievable horror, as they saw on TV first one and then the other tower crumble before their eyes. By now some of their neighbours from the other apartments had taken advantage of the open door and were standing in the room with them. All were numbed with shock. Elena was moaning quiet soft moans whilst Christina wanted to scream. She kept trying Robert's cell-phone number but was getting no reply. He had said he was going to call back.

'Please God. Please God. For the children, if not for me.'

Someone thrust a glass of their own special cognac into her hand. They had found the bottle in her cupboard. Without thinking, or even looking, she gulped it down. It was burning her throat but that did not matter. What mattered was that the Twin Towers had been burning and now those same towers where her husband was, those towers that were the symbol of modern New York and all it stood for, were no more.

One by one the others in the room quietly slipped away, their own minds full of thoughts and fears for their own loved ones. For each and every one who had stood there watching their known world had just disintegrated before their eyes. Thought upon thought flashed before them. What was happening and how many had survived? And above all the questions 'Who?' and 'Why?'.

Left alone Christina and Elena looked at each other, barely able to get a word out.

Elena finally managed to utter, 'What do we do?'

They had seen pictures of a cloud of choking smoke – almost a ball of smoke – rolling into mid-town with folk fleeing before it. Again the questions 'Who?' and 'Why?' and then the dreadful thought started to creep its way through their brains, 'Is there more to come?'

The phone rang, breaking the silence that surrounded the ever-chattering TV commentators. It was James, Robert's father, calling from Rhode Island.

'Have you seen the TV?' he asked. 'Helen here is worried. Where is Robert today? Did he go to Albany yesterday as planned?'

'No,' she replied. There was a long pause. Christina could scarcely get the words out.

'He…was…in there. I spoke with him only half an hour ago…'

She could say no more. Tears were running down her face.

'Hi, are you still there?' There was almost a tremor of desperation coming down the line from Providence. 'Are you still there?'

Elena took the phone gently from Christina.

'She is still here, we both are, but we do not know about our men.'

She hung up.

CHAPTER II

Into an unknown world

Up in Providence, in the sumptuous home that he and Helen occupied thanks to his post as a Professor of Psychiatry, James also put the phone down.

He had just started to run through his notes for the afternoon lecture on the behaviour of the unemployed during the great Depression of the 1930s when Helen had called him urgently to come back into the kitchen and look at the TV News. Breakfast had been a bit late that morning as Helen was in no hurry. She was due to go down to Newport to have lunch with an old friend who was having a late holiday in the area. But that was not until later so she had sat down with an extra coffee whilst James had got dressed and then disappeared into his study.

Helen and James had had a good life since they had married in 1968. He was now 58 and she was four years his junior. They had met at Columbia when he was majoring in psychiatry and she in marketing. Her professor had recently returned from a lecture tour in London England and had regaled his students with stories of the Brits and their odd ideas of everything from working hours and class-distinction in the office to dirty trains and warm beer. The students had lapped it all up and indeed the series of lectures had been so popular at Columbia that they had been attended by students from other disciplines.

It was at one of those lectures that Helen had spotted the gawky 25 year old psychiatry student with blond hair who was laughing his head off on the other side of the room. Her own reactions to the stories from far-off London had at the same time caught the eye of that young man as he had studied the responses of his fellow students. On the way out he had asked her to have a coffee with him. The following Saturday they went to a dance.

There was a spark there when they were together and they never looked back. Indeed they had been supremely happy together bringing up their children and leading their individual lives and job careers until that fateful morning of September 11th 2001 when smoke poured out of the Twin Towers and they saw their world collapsing in front of them.

Somehow, down in Manhattan, Christina survived the hours, weeks and months that followed that terrible day that had started with such high hopes. It had been a typical New York September day, a Tuesday and only just a week after they had all been up in Providence with Robert's parents for the Labor Day holiday weekend.

People had returned to town from their long vacations, the schools had started the new term and the city parks and squares had been gently dozing in the warm late-summer sun under a blue sky. There had promised to be a few weeks of lull before the social calendar got into gear and talk would be of the opera at the Met, of the latest shows on Broadway and of who had been invited to which and whose dinner parties and dances.

Instead it was destined to be a day when the greatest city on earth was to resemble a funeral pyre, with plumes of smoke spiralling up into the heavens high above a citizenry, half of whom were so stunned that they had begun to believe the world was coming to an end.

At first for Christina, for her parents-in-law James and Helen, and for so many others it was a period of sheer disbelief. Disbelief that such a thing could happen anywhere in the world and above all in New York and its very heart of Manhattan. To the older generation such as James and Helen such a possibility might have been credible twenty or thirty years previously at the height of the Cold War; but all that was supposed to have been a thing of the past. Had the West been deluded? Was this really the start of the often-forecast final Armageddon?

The first instinct up in Providence was that James and Helen should drive down to Manhattan to look after Christina and those two beautiful grand-children. Yet they could not do so for Mayor Giuliani had closed all the bridges and tunnels into the island of Manhattan. They could not get in, and Christina would not be able to get out with George and baby Maria.

Nor if the truth was known did Christina want to leave New York just now. She, like so many others, spent day after day, almost half-comatose yet with a purpose, for she still believed in her heart that Robert was out there. Perhaps he had been knocked unconscious and lost his memory? Maybe he was walking up and down looking for her? Or at least perhaps he had been buried alive under all that rubble but in a pocket of air and they would find him. Perhaps he had been rescued by those wonderful First Responders, the Fire and Police, and was somewhere in a hospital bed?

So day after mid-September day, Christina left the children with Rosa and walked up and down the streets. Looking at every passing face and stopping passers-by, many of whom were doing the same searching for their own loved-ones; but always receiving the same sad, half-mumbled reply, 'Sorry. No I have not seen him.'

She wore round her neck a makeshift picture of Robert. It was strung from a necklace of Venetian glass that her beloved Robert had bought for her when they had been in that city. He had purchased it on a stall near the Rialto bridge.

The old vendor had smiled at her and said 'Bella fortuna Signora' – 'good luck madam' – when he had handed it to her.

Now that luck was needed more than ever before. Would it bring back Robert to her? How often during those days that followed did Christina want that old shopkeeper to be right?

As soon as the bridges were open again James brought Helen down to help care for the children. It was a delicate time for all in the apartment. The children wanted to know why their father had not come home each evening. Christina was in a semi-permanent daze and Helen could only fill the emptiness in her own heart by helping to occupy the children with books, games and cuddly toys.

For James the answer had to be a stiff upper-lip and an application of self-discipline in the way they lived for now. Each morning he would go out with Christina, knowing in his heart of hearts that their searches were futile. But he was determined to finally reach the stage that his daughter-in-law would eventually come to her own conclusion that there was no more that could be done. His military experience told him that they should cover each of the north-south "avenues" one day and then the next to walk one of the east-west running "streets". At least New York's grid layout made the searching just a tiny bit easier.

They started in the Upper East Side at 78th Street. It was a long way from Ground Zero but Robert could be anywhere in that vast city and maybe some homing-instinct would guide him towards his old home?

As the days turned into weeks and the weeks became further and further away from that day of days the whole family – what was left of it – came little by little to recognise the futility of their hopes. There were nightly outpourings on the TV of stories of human tragedy but somehow their own little family-gathering found it hard to concentrate on the suffering of others and the "off-switch" was frequently in use.

There were services of commemoration and visits by dignitaries from other countries all anxious to show their support for the USA in its time of desolation. For a few with long memories it had been the greatest shock for their nation since Pearl Harbour; whilst for those who had grown up since the end of World War Two it was simply unbelievable that anyone could do such a thing to their own United States and get away with it.

Behind all this anguish and very real anger, lay in the back of so many minds the fear that tomorrow, or next day or next week, these people would strike again. Would they target the Big Apple again? Would they have a more successful attempt at The Pentagon next time? Or even perhaps the next attack would be over in San Francisco or Los Angeles? The fear of uncertainty hung like a heavy drape over every morning as September faded into October; and before long it would be Christmas. If they could bear Christmas this year. But they had to think of the children.

CHAPTER III

England 1849

Slowly, very slowly, Robert pulled the heavy blanket down from over his face and opened his eyes. The English air beyond the blanket was cold and he could see patterns of ice on the inside of the window-pane. 'Jack Frost has been at his work again,' he thought as he looked at the wonderful designs that the overnight cold air had traced on the inside of the glass.

It was five o'clock on a November morning in the Year of Our Lord 1849, and it was time for Robert George Jackson to arise. Indeed it was time for him to go through to the smithy next door and start to stir the overnight embers, to throw on a few logs of beech wood, and to get the fire going so that by half-past six his father James could commence his own work as the village blacksmith. If Robert did not have that fire up to the required heat in time for James then the first horse that turned up to be shod, or the emergency wheel repair that was needed by a local carter, would be delayed, and that was not good for business.

Robert's feet touched the earthen floor, reluctantly he dressed, pulling his smock over his shoulders and hauling up his trousers before tying them with a piece of old twine. He headed for the pump in the yard. There was nothing better to bring a nineteen-year-old into the realms of the working day than a good dose of cold water over his face and the nape of his neck. And he would soon dry himself in front of those still-red embers.

By time his father appeared twenty minutes later to check all was well Robert had had the bellows blowing up those embers that had lain smouldering away overnight and there was a healthy glow of orange-red that was spreading under the working surface of the fire. By half past five, James had pronounced that he was satisfied and father and son headed back into the kitchen for breakfast. Four large slices of ham from the pig they had slaughtered at the back-end of the summer, three good thick slices of bread fried in the pig-lard and some mashed potato. That was the sort of English breakfast that a man needed before a twelve hour day of work at the anvil, or a boy needed at working the bellows over the working surface of the fire.

Without a good strong heat his father would easily fly into a rage if he could not temper the iron or shape the horseshoes with the first couple of blows of his hammer or rasps of his file. If the metal was not at the required temperature it would be Robert who would receive a cuff on the ears.

The nineteen-year-old was on his second plate of ham and fried-bread when his sister appeared but he scarcely looked up to greet her. Sophie was two years his senior and any other man of nineteen with good blood in his veins would have immediately been drawn by her magnetism and her looks. But brothers were brothers and sisters were only sisters. So the finely shaped breasts that led the twenty-one year old forward, and the flaxen hair that she always kept neatly tied in a bun on the top of her head, meant but little to a lad who had to concentrate on the furnace being right in time for his father to pick up the hammer and set to work. Robert grunted at Sophie, swallowed a glass of water from the cream earthenware jug, and started for the smithy next door.

'Well my love,' said Anne Jackson as she took in her daughter with a glance before clearing away the tin plates and wooden platters on the kitchen table.

'Well my love, you be comin' to market with me today?'

She knew the answer would be in the affirmative before she asked the question. Sophie would not miss a chance to go to the Thursday Market in nearby Stonefield unless the town was smitten with yet another plague of cholera. After all Nathaniel would be there selling his father's produce at their family stall in the square; and Nathaniel's eyes lit up every time Sophie appeared.

Anne had seen the exchange of their glances more than once. And then there had been that night last summer, just after their beautiful daughter had attained her majority, when she had come in a little flustered from visiting Nat's father's farm. Anne had sent her over to buy some eggs and it would not normally have taken five hours to walk the two miles to Windle Farm, buy the eggs, and return. But it had been a lovely summers' evening, one of those days when the air was warm, the corn was ripening quickly and the hay was already gathered in. Sophie had still a few wisps of hay sticking from behind the bun in her hair when she arrived back and Anne had wondered whether that red flush was just one of walking back fast with the eggs or whether some haystack had proved a comforting venue for her daughter and Nat for an hour or two on that beautiful English summer's evening.

Anyway, today was Thursday and it would be all hustle and bustle at the market so they must be off by half seven to walk the four miles into town and do their shopping. Anne gathered her apron round her waist, tied the knot yet again and set-to with first washing-up the platters and then after that she had a couple of the mens' smocks to mend. It was Sophie's job to sweep the floor with the besom and to peg the clothes out on the line in the yard.

There were a few clouds in the sky and there might be the odd shower before they got back. So they had best take their heavy woollen capes. Four miles walking with a chill wind coming down off the hills could be no fun. A quick visit to the privy at the end of the yard and where Robert had just been putting some of the over-night ashes to keep it "sweet" and all was ready. Anne and her tall blonde daughter were ready for market.

As they set off the first horse, a great big "Shire" from a farm at the far end of the village was already emerging from the smithy with its new shoes; and ready for a day in harness before the plough. Another was waiting it's turn in the yard outside, slaking it's thirst from the large red-stone trough especially kept for the day's customers.

No one could describe the town of Stonefield as "pretty". A pretty good place to live and to work maybe but not pretty in the aesthetic sense. It was a mill-town at the foot of the "Backbone of England", that range of rolling limestone hills that ran down the middle of Northern England and whose streams provided water power for the cotton, wool and silk mills that meant employment in the large number of small towns that clustered at the feet of both sides of the range.

To the west of those Pennine Hills lay the cotton towns that centred upon the growing metropolis of Manchester; whilst to the east were those that concentrated on wool and which came together in the focal point of Leeds. South of Manchester cotton had failed to take its grip on the small towns that had developed and instead silk was the main employer. But the future of silk seemed less sure than that of cotton.

"King Cotton" was certainly the industry of the future. Large bales of it were everywhere to be seen in those towns. Most of it came from America by ship to the port of Liverpool and then by the new railways to the various towns, where it was loaded on carts to be driven to the different mills.

However Stonefield was one of those towns that relied on silk and there were over twenty mills in the town. The mills were easily recognised with their big, some thought ugly, red brick buildings. Each had a tall tower in one corner that served as the column for the stairs up which mill workers clambered each morning to their appropriate floors and down which during the day came the bales of cloth, reels of ribbons and all the other products that typified this industrial heartland of the centre of the British Empire. At each of the mills there was a large chimney that all day, except on the Sabbath, belched out smoke over the town.

On those days from September onwards, when the air started to cool and the mists began to roll in across the Cheshire Plain, the sulphurous smoke began to gather in thick layers between the rows and rows of new red brick houses that had recently been built to accommodate the families who had moved into the towns to seek work and escape the rural depression that lay all around. On those same days, no shirt or smock that was put out to dry in a sparkling white condition would come back in without a thin layer of black grime on the collar or the cuffs. It was a battle that every housewife knew she could not win.

It was Robert's duty each morning to take back to the various mills the wheels, the joining-bars and the many other items that James had repaired the previous day. They had a handcart in the yard and this was used whenever their day's load included one of those large iron wheels that operated the leather belts in the ceilings of the mills and which enabled the power to be spread all over the building. Those wheels were heavy and if a mill lay at the top of a hill it took all the energy that Robert had to push the cart to the mill gates and deliver his load. Whether it be a worn spindle or a fractured crankshaft it had to be returned to its owner before eight in the morning and the previous day's casualties collected for James to work on after lunch.

It was when visiting the "Kent" mill, named after the Duke of Kent who had been the father of the present Queen Victoria (her predecessor, King William had left no legitimate children to succeed to the throne), that Robert had met Caroline Williams. It had been a cold winter's day and the puddles of water from the previous day had turned to ice overnight. Caroline had been on her way back to the village where she lived with her mother and father when she slipped and bruised her ankle. Robert had, from some distance behind, already been admiring those ankles peeping below the long brown skirt when he saw her fall over. Putting down the cart he had rushed forward and helped her to her feet. The poor girl had been unable to take more than a few steps so Robert had thrown an old sack over the half dozen pieces of ironwork he had already collected and had lifted her onto the cart and pushed her home.

Despite the pain she was in Robert had seen a glint in the girl's eye when he had carried her into the care of her mother. Not one to miss his chances with the fair sex he had asked permission to call next day to see how she had fared. It was curious how almost every day after that, until her ankle was able to take the strain, Robert found his deliveries took him through her village. Every day that was until they were both able to meet up along some country lane, or one or other of them knew of a derelict barn where they could shelter from the winter cold and keep each other warm.

It was just before Easter in The Year of Our Lord 1852 that the twenty-one year old Robert George Jackson and Caroline Williams exchanged marriage vows before the Revd. Thomas Forsyth in the 14th century parish church of St Werburgh. The wedding service was on a beautiful English spring day. Outside the church the sun was shining under a blue sky and casting strong shadows from the family gravestones that surrounded the ancient red-sandstone building. In Cheshire almost every parish church had been built with that local stone, as had many of the walls that surrounded the parks and gardens of the local great houses.

The village was agog with excitement. The English flag of St George was flying on the church tower and the old lych-gate to the church had been festooned with greenery by her friends long before Caroline stepped down from the cart and walked into the church whilst tightly gripping her father's arm. Already standing at the front of the nave before the altar Robert could not resist turning his head as the boy at the organ pump started up the bellows and the music commenced to waft through the filled church. Tears crept into his eyes as Robert saw walking

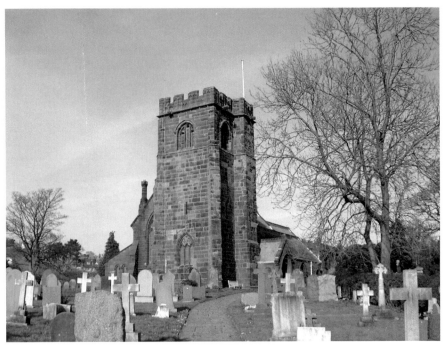

A typical red-sandstone Cheshire church surrounded by the graves of past generations.
Photo by Peter Pennington

up to him, ever so slowly, a beautiful White Angel. A White Angel that was to be with him in body, mind and spirit for the rest of his days.

Soon after their first married Christmas she was with child and by that October the name "George James Jackson" had already appeared on the parish register of births showing "date of birth 21st October 1853". That was Trafalgar Day when the nation annually celebrated Admiral Nelson's success in defeating the French Navy way back in 1805. The following Sunday the new-born child was baptised in the village church.

The year after that important Trafalgar Day event there took place another important happening in the lives of Robert, Caroline and little George James Jackson. Important not just because another baby was on the way but because the parents were to take what was to be perhaps the biggest decision of their lives. They were to leave England behind and set sail for America.

The England in which they lived was in a restless state. First of all there had been the Chartists, a political movement with its demands for all men to have a vote not just those who held property. These extremists were also demanding annual parliaments although that itself meant little to Robert and Caroline. Anyway, as far as Caroline was concerned, politics was "mens' business". It was nothing to do with women. Maybe one day long in the future women might possibly also be able to vote, but like drinking beer in an alehouse or playing cricket, it was nothing to do with the fair sex. Women had enough to do with producing and caring for children and keeping the house clean with good food on the table.

But these Chartist people were not the only unsettling thing. There had been revolutions all over Europe in the last few years. In France the King had been overthrown in yet another uprising. Even in their own English countryside the farmers were up in revolt against the change in the price of corn and the danger of farmers losing their markets to cheap imports of wheat. "Repeal of the Corn Laws" Robert had said it was called, and all due to the same Prime Minster who had once started a police force that was called "Peelers" after him.

If the farmers could not sell their crops then they did not need to have their horses shod, nor could they pay for the work if it had to be done. There was no doubt that recently the amount of work had dropped in the forge and sometimes Robert had to explain to Caroline that his father had only given him a few shillings that week. Less money from the smithy meant that in turn Caroline could not buy ribbons from the drapers near the mill down the road. It seemed an ever-lasting circle and many folk were getting depressed. Some people had left Stonefield and gone to look for work in Manchester or the big port of Liverpool but they often came back with tales that the best labouring jobs had been taken by Irishmen escaping from their own potato famine in that country. These "Paddys" were even getting jobs in the mills and that meant good English men and women were out of work.

There was also another breeze blowing in the air and it was one of stories of great wealth that could be earned in countries like America and Australia. The magic word that always came up was "gold". Those countries seemed to be made of it. Everyone knew someone who had gone to California or to the colony of Victoria in Australia and had made it rich by digging for gold. There was even that chap who lived a few doors down the road near Robert's mother and father. He had left his family behind and went to Liverpool where he signed on as a member of a ship's crew and worked his passage to New York. Some said he was now very wealthy and would soon be sending for his wife and seven children to join him. Some had muttered darkly that the poor chap might get a big surprise if he found nine, not seven, children arrived on the ship, the way his wife had been carrying-on after he left.

Often on a Saturday evening Robert and Caroline would discuss these tales of far-off riches and bit by bit, week by week, they each began to wonder to themselves how the other would respond if they suggested trying their own luck in the colonies or in America.

The first stories of gold being discovered in California – wherever that was – had been reported in 1849 just before Robert had come to the rescue of that lovely girl with attractive ankles who was walking ahead of him one winter's day. Later there were stories that in Australia the gold was lying on the ground and in river-beds just waiting to be picked up and to make one rich.

These stories of riches, and the fever and temptations they inspired those still at home, had even infected the older generation. But James and Anne were themselves too old to think of emigrating or the creating of a new life in another country however fascinating the temptations of great wealth. However they were not the sort of parents to stand in the way of their children.

At first when the youngsters announced their intentions one beautiful summer evening the parents sighed but contented themselves with the thought that they would still have Sophie with them and that maybe before long they would be welcoming young Nathaniel into the family. Perhaps he would replace Robert and take over the smithy in due course? They would have to wait and see. Then a few weeks after they had learned of their son's plans his sister announced that she and Nathaniel had also decided to seek their fortune overseas and that they would accompany Robert and Caroline to America. This had been very hard news to bear for now the future of the smithy would devolve on young Joshua and who was still only eleven years of age.

From thence-forward it was all a matter of planning. To Robert and Caroline fell the responsibility of finding how to go to their new chosen-land whilst for Nat and Sophie there was the little matter of getting married.

For some time now the papers had been full of reports, based on letters back home to parents, telling of good fortunes but also of sadnesses. Letters had told of journeys across America by train and wagon, of new homes built on virgin land and of the misfortunes of those who never got beyond the ports of New York and Boston where they first landed.

Old George Johnson who lived at Elm Tree Farm down by the river had told James and Anne that he had received a letter from his son Zeb who had "struck it rich" in California. Old George himself could not swear that that was what Zeb had said, as he himself could not read, but the innkeeper at the Royal Oak Inn where the London Coach used to call in the old days before the coming of the new railway, had read the letter for George and had said this was what was in it. On the way back from the inn that evening Old George had met the vicar – the Reverend Mr Forsyth – and George had shown him the letter. Next Sunday the morning service included a prayer for the safety of all those from the villages and nearby farms who had left England's shores for a life of adventure overseas. Like the innkeeper, the vicar had decided that when he read the letter and found out that Zeb in fact had died when the walls of the gold mine had collapsed according to the writer, it would not be kind to tell the old man for he himself had little time left on this earth and he would have grieved sorely to the end of his days.

The more Robert and Caroline talked the less they liked the prospect of California. First there would be the long sail to New York, then the railway for the next part of the journey and eventually those wagon adventures through dangerous country until they arrived in the land of gold and plenty. Was it really necessary to go all that way? And was it morally right to put all their lives at risk, especially that of little George James and his future brother or sister? As an infant the small child would have enough odds to fight against in trying to reach adulthood, so why pile on the risks? Would there not be good enough jobs in the first part of America that they would reach? At least they could try there first on landing.

CHAPTER IV

Letting go the ropes

Looking back it had of course been in the spring of the Year of the Lord 1852 that twenty-one-year-old Robert George Jackson had married his nineteen-year-old bride. Then not long afterwards Caroline had been with-child. George James Jackson, a bawling seven-pound infant, had first blinked his eyes on the world on 21st October 1853 and since then the days and months seem to have flown past and it was time to start their great adventure.

The fields had turned a golden yellow early the following year of 1854 in the North of England. The stooks of corn sheaves were lined up in neat rows of small pyramids as Robert and Caroline set off for the local railway station to get the train to the port of Liverpool. Nat and Sophie had gone ahead two days before to ensure that all the trunks arrived safely at the dockside. Herbert, the village carter, had said that his old nag would take three days to make the trip with all their belongings. Whether he made it in three or even four or five would depend on the strength of the local ale he found when he stopped each night, turning the horse loose and sleeping under the cart. So Nat and Sophie had offered to go ahead as there was no guarantee what Herbert would get up to once he found himself amongst the beggars, peddlers and whores that were the common currency of every great port. They had all arranged to stay with some cousins of Nat's in the village of Toxteth on the outskirts of Liverpool.

Now Robert and Caroline were to join them there later that evening as they cast their eyes back on the so-familiar fields with those little stooks of golden yellow. Funny how the wheat for bread-making always ripened before the oats that were needed to feed the horses. If it was a wet summer then the oats never ripened at all and the horses on the farms faced a lean and hungry winter ahead of them.

Robert spotted a tear or two in the corners of Caroline's eyes as she gazed at the wheat and beyond at the cows grazing on the lush green Cheshire grass, filling their udders with beautiful creamy milk that would poor into the pails when they returned to the shippons for milking that evening. It was often said that the beautiful Cheshire cheese for which the county was so famous was because those cows ate grass that had absorbed little bits of the great big old salt lake that lay beneath those fields. Would they ever again be able to enjoy a slab of some of that delicious crumbly white or pink (the locals called them "plain" or "coloured") cheese on a piece of bread when they reached their new homes the other side of the Atlantic? Soon those small Cheshire fields of corn or cows would only be a memory. So would the squat red-sandstone church tower with its flag of St George still flying proudly from dawn to dusk each day. It would be funny in the future living under a different flag – but they would always remember their English roots, and be proud of them.

Before long the tower of St Werburgh's church where they had been married had dropped behind the copse of elm trees at the corner. Both their minds were floating back to that wonderful day and all that had led up to it. For weeks before,

Caroline had dreamed of a fine white dress with its veil that had been handed down from generation to generation.

Her grandmother had claimed that her own mother had worn the same veil at her wedding the year that Bonnie Prince Charlie had invaded England with all his wild Scotsmen, and when they had passed through the town on the way south. Family folklore said they had been a frightening army of red whiskered men in skirts. For their music they had played on some form of pipes that protruded out of bags made from the stomachs of Scottish sheep. The joke had been that the music was enough to make the stomachs of English sheep who heard them churn. Folk in the town said that no respectable young English maiden had been safe that day from the northern marauders. Then only a few weeks later the rag-tag of an army had streamed back through the town, dejected and forlorn. It was hastening back to the mountains and glens whence they had come, in order to get in their own harvests before the Scottish winter would set in.

A little more than a century later Caroline had walked up the same aisle as her great grandmother. But surely no wedding ever could have been as wonderful as Caroline's own to Robert? How they had both been looking forward to the day. No longer would they need to take long evening walks searching for a convenient haystack or a field with tall grass that could seclude them from prying eyes. Instead the Vicar, Mr Forsyth, seemed to have just the right words in his address and afterwards, before Caroline had climbed into the cart that was to take them to the inn for the wedding breakfast, the old clergyman had given her a big hug and whispered in her ear that she was the most pretty bride he had ever married.

Later her new husband had told her she was a White Angel, the greatest and most sincere compliment that any lover could give to a girl that meant so much to him.

But today it was no good thinking like this. They had a future to look forward to, and Liverpool with its ships and the sea beyond would be with them before that very nightfall.

The cart in which they were travelling to the local railway station had been decked out with ribbons and wild flowers that had been plucked that very morning from the hedgerows by some of Caroline's friends. The two Shire horses had all their brasses gleaming and wore red, white and blue ribbons about their ears. Robert had pointed out that the same three colours were used both for the British flag and for that of their new home, the United States of America.

The train journey was a slow and tedious one and they had to change at the old city of Chester, an ancient city which still had standing its original walls and gates, guarding the city first built by the Romans. Robert had been there once before when he had wandered round the ancient cathedral and had then strolled through the market place where he had bought from a farmer's stall some of that wonderful "Cheshire cheese" for which the county was so famous. Afterwards he had admired some of the ancient buildings with their black and white timbered frames. In Robert's grandfather's time Chester, at the head of the estuary of the river Dee, had still been the traditional port for Ireland from where the packet-boats had set out for Dublin. He had had his lunch at an inn called just that, "The Dublin Packet". But by now the river was starting to silt up and the trade had moved to nearby Liverpool where the fast-flowing waters of the river Mersey had ensured there would not be a build-up of silt in the same way.

Liverpool was on the opposite bank of the Mersey and so Robert and Caroline had to travel by train to Birkenhead on the Cheshire side of the river and then cross by ferry. The little cutter which took them over was crowded with other would-be emigrants and its captain had great difficulty manoeuvring between the large clippers and other sailing vessels, laden with produce from all over the world, which lay at anchor awaiting a berth or were preparing to sally forth to foreign lands. From the little crowded ferry it was almost impossible to see the sky so many were the tall masts that dominated the skyline. After fifty minutes struggle the cutter finally tied up and Robert and Caroline found Sophie and Nat waiting for them at the top of the steps.

Next morning the two young couples breakfasted well with their Liverpool hosts before setting off for the docks. Robert had never seen such a city before. The previous evening as they had made their way from the ferry to the Toxteth home of their cousins they had passed row upon row of neatly-built red brick houses. All those houses had gone up over the past few years to accommodate the tens of thousands who had left their old cottages in the countryside and had headed to Liverpool to find employment in the factories and docks and which were then being created by the wealth resulting from the new port. These houses were very different to the country cottages to which Robert was accustomed. To start with they had no gardens to grow vegetables for the pot. Then they were in long rows, and so squashed together that they had a second storey on top of the front room and kitchen. He wondered if they were as warm in winter as his old home with a straw-thatch roof? At the back of each row was a long narrow alley but before reaching the gate to it each house had its privy only a few yards from the back door. At least in the dark of winter it wouldn't be so far to go in the middle of the night! Then there were also to be seen in Liverpool the great big public buildings which seemed to be going up all over the place, some of which they passed as they went down to the docks.

The view that morning, as the two young couples really saw the river in all its majesty for the first time, was truly breathtaking. When they had first arrived by train and then crossed over in the ferry they had been too tired to take it all in and the little ferry had been so crowded. However now it was all before them. A wide, wide river with the town of Birkenhead on the opposite shore. A stately clipper, her sails now folded because she was being guided along by a paddle steamer tug, was in mid-stream. Her name "Constance" could be seen painted at her bow. Someone told them she had just arrived from China with a load of tea. She had sailed from Liverpool firstly to Australia with emigrants heading for the gold mines there and had then proceeded to China to collect the tea for the return journey. It seemed as if the whole world was on the move. There were empty emigrant vessels at anchor in midstream awaiting their opportunity to go into dock and take on passengers for Australia, for New Zealand, for Canada and for America. One of them must be theirs, but which one?

They wondered if their own vessel was amongst those tugging at their anchors against the fast flowing tide. A river which was carrying all sorts of flotsam and jetsam as the waters rushed towards the open sea beyond. There were barges towed by paddle steamers and low in the water with supplies of cotton from the United States. "King Cotton" was the ruler of the county of Lancashire. They could tell that some of those ships were American because of the flag they were flying. Nat looked hard at that flag with its red and white stripes and some stars tucked into one corner. He wondered how familiar it might be to them all in the future.

Then there were small colliers low in the water as they headed for the mouth of the river full of Lancashire's own coal and destined for the jute mills of India. With his own knowledge of the weight of coal gained from many days in the smithy at home Robert marvelled that such little ships could survive many months of gales and storms before they arrived in some far-off port. Somebody told him that often those colliers were taking their loads to places such as Mauritius or the Cape of Good Hope, wherever those were, and where the big new passenger steamships could re-fuel for the next part of their voyages to China, India and other lands.

Darting in between all the majestic ships were little ferries, their sails trimmed to the winds as they plied between the two banks of the river with passengers. As they watched one made a fairly quick passage to the Birkenhead shore opposite whilst another with only a handful of intrepid travellers was making a much more laborious effort to get upstream to somewhere called Eastham. Robert espied a cow also being carried on that tiny vessel. 'Did cows get sea-sick?' he wondered. Anyway how would they all feel once they were on board ship and off to New York?

Finding "their" dock was not easy. Everyone they asked seemed to be new to the city. Some, even if they had told them the right answer, could not be understood because of their accents. English accents seemed to be in a minority with Irish and Scottish Gaelic tongues vying with Welsh where every word seemed to start with a funny sort of "ll". He had heard that Welsh language before when in Chester market. Chester was only about two miles from the Welsh border.

Eventually the dock gate was reached. The wives were left with James and Ann who had arrived earlier in the day to bid them farewell; and who had accompanied them down to the dockside whilst the other parents had stayed back with the cousins in Toxteth. At the dock gate the two young men were allowed to go through by the policeman on duty. It did not take long for Robert and Nat to find the dock office. There, after standing in a queue, they were able to satisfy themselves that their trunks and boxes had arrived safely. They paid the remainder of their passage money and in return were told where to find their ship.

An hour later the two men returned to the dock gate to find their families sitting on a pile of packing cases patiently awaiting their news. They told them it was both good and bad. The good was that their passages were confirmed and their berths allocated. The bad news was that they would have to wait two more days before going on board – and they had been warned there might be a further couple of days at anchor in the river before the clearance orders were given for the ship to sail.

Those next couple of days were very special for all concerned in both families. The women visited the shops and markets of this large cosmopolitan city. They visited milliners for extra bonnets "just in case one was blown into the sea" and to a draper to buy another corset for Caroline. A haberdasher was also on the list of shops visited. The two mothers bought little "extras" for their dear departing daughters whilst the fathers indulged in ensuring their sons were well-acquainted with the taverns and the local ales before they set off on their great adventure.

At the end of their last night on English soil Caroline snuggled up to Robert beneath the quilt and gently confessed to him that she had been rather extravagant in the last two days. She had lashed out and reduced their savings by one pound four shillings and two pence-halfpenny. Robert forgave her, not daring to admit that Liverpool brews were somewhat more expensive than back home and that he himself had not stinted his contribution to the male drinking-pot fund.

One good excuse for visiting the various ale houses around the docks had been their competition of espying a vessel, whether tied up at the quayside or at anchor in the river, then guessing whence it had come or to where it was bound. It was then "essential" that they sought confirmation of their guesses at the nearest inn. By the time the final night on shore arrived both young men were prepared to sail round the world; to all parts, both Empire and foreign, and to put the local inhabitants aright on all matters political and religious! "The Health" of that pretty young woman, "Her Majesty, Queen Victoria" had been toasted so often that she was bound to live for at least another half-century.

As the Thursday morning dawned there was a steady drizzle on the Liverpool streets. Men headed for work with their collars pulled up to stop the rain running down their necks. The poor who had spent their nights on the doorsteps of the more wealthy inhabitants of streets lived in by families such as the Gladstones shuffled off in the hope of finding the remnants of last night's dinner-parties still lying in the refuse barrels outside the back doors. Scholars dragged their reluctant feet towards a day of learning be it at dame school or academy or the nearest "British School". Yet despite the drizzle and the poverty all around it was not a bad day to be their last on English soil; for to them at least the two young couples could look forward to adventure and an exciting future. They were off to America, where men were free to make their fortunes and where all were equal without the heavy hand of class distinction; or even still, the remote chance of transportation for the honest stealing of a rabbit for the Sunday pot.

The queue – they were soon to have to use the American term "line-up", but that was in the future – at the dock office was long and without shelter from the steady rain. Family by family they moved forward to the clerk at the table and presented their papers certifying that the passage money had been paid. Every name was entered in full on the Passenger List. Not just their names but also their age and gender and for the men their occupation. English, Scots, Welsh and Irish were all shown by their home nations. Just in front was a family of father, mother and three small girls and with a young baby brother cradled in his mother's arms. Upon being asked his nationality the tall man, with fair hair and a long unruly moustache, explained they were from Sweden and had come by train from Hull the previous day.

'Foreign Parts, then,' decided the clerk, adding that, 'We don't want no turnip-heads in our books. If you isn't British then you is Foreign.'

Such was the England that Robert and Caroline, Sophie and Nat, were about to leave. You were Upper class or Working class. You were British or Foreign and if by any mischance of birth you were not fair-skinned then you really did not count at all.

Before leaving the clerk's desk each person, man or woman, child or infant, was given a wooden tag on a leather cord to hang around their neck. "Carthage", the name of their ship, and a number, were carved into the round disc. The number indicated their berth.

Collecting their boxes from the depository the two young men and James between them struggled along the quayside until they found their temporary future home. Stepping over ropes that seemed everywhere and avoiding pools of water on the stone flags of the dockside, the men eventually managed to come to a halt at the foot of the companionway to the ship.

All around, and in between the milling throng of would-be emigrants, there wove what seemed to be hundreds of vendors and sharpsters. Some were selling fruit and drinks to those both waiting to go on board and to those who were to stay on-shore. Other men offered to carry the packing cases, trunks and boxes on board for a couple of pence or to run back into town to obtain last-minute purchases for those who had now suddenly remembered that this or that was packed in the wrong box and would be down in the hold and so not available for use on board. Whether the change from money given to those who were offering such a purchasing service would ever been see again – let alone the required goods or its conveyor – was a moot point. One trusting lady, Sophie noticed, gave a tall thin individual with a red spotted neckerchief and moleskin trousers, two shillings to go and purchase an extra bonnet for her teenage daughter. She must remember to ask the lady in a day or so whether the bonnet ever appeared.

Accompanied by their curious parents it was not long before the two couples found their berths amongst a row on the "larboard" or "left" side of the vessel. The wooden cots were narrow and just long enough to get one's head down at night. Caroline herself would have to share hers with little George, and of course in her condition how would she be able to cope if there were any storms? The horrible thing was that the bottom of the cot above was only some eighteen inches above one's face. Caroline mused, with a smile on her face, as to what would happen to a fat man or women, especially if once wedged in at night they would have to get out in an emergency. On the other hand any corpulent person would not fall out when the vessel rolled! Ah well, you could not have it all ways.

Then there were the final farewells. Hugs and kisses all round and of course not an eye was dry as parents and offspring held hands for the last time before they were to be separated perhaps for ever. Never had more promises been made to write so many letters, never so many exhortations made to look after one another. Seldom were so many assurances uttered with the unspoken thought that they would never be kept and that they would perhaps never all meet again. But the physical bonds had to be broken, the hand unclasped and the kerchiefs used to wipe the eyes. The future had to be faced by all.

As James and Anne Jackson, Charles and Hannah Williams and Nat's parents all stood on the quayside the last ropes were lifted off the bollards and dropped into the water. The final umbilical cord from the bow was tossed onto the land and the paddle-tug hooted her warning as she took up the strain and started to move the "Carthage" out into the river. Was it chance, or was it an omen, that for the first time that day the clouds parted and a strong ray of sun beamed down upon all those gathered at the side of the ship as they gave two huzzahs to their friends and relatives on shore. The responding reply was a shade muted, doubtless due to so many throats being dry and voices cracking with emotions that were now being allowed to come to the surface once they could not be seen by the adventurers on the ship.

The following morning there was a buzz of excitement all over the ship. They had all been told to be on board the previous evening before dusk and the ship had then slipped out into the middle of the river and dropped anchor. Most of the emigrants had enjoyed what was to prove their last night of peaceful sleep without the continual lap, lap of water passing beneath the keel for many a night to come. It had been late when the men had turned in after a final smoke on deck. The tide had been flowing in from the open sea beyond the mouth of the river so the anchor at the bow had resulted in them facing down-stream and the city of Liverpool had been on the "right" side as Robert still insisted on calling it. By the time they were first up the tide had turned and now the city was on the other side of the ship as she swung at her anchor chain.

It seemed funny to these good country-folk passengers, many of whom had never before seen the sea or even a river as large as this, that all the ships seemed to move together with their bows first pointing one way and then another, according to the flow of the river as influenced by the tide. Near them was a Black Ball Line emigrant ship. She, someone had told them, went to Hobson's Bay, wherever that was, in Australia. They had considered Australia as an alternative to America but they had decided against it.

Half way through the morning the watchers on the "Carthage" saw the first of the sails at the top masts on the Australian-bound vessel being broken out and a tug taking aboard a tow rope. There was a high pitched squeal from the latter as the paddles started to turn and little by little she started to get underway and head down stream with her charge in tow.

Then after they had all been down below for their lunch in their little mess groups they had washed and put away their plates and utensils and gone back up on deck to watch life. It was Caroline who first spotted a tug heading towards their very own ship. At the front of the vessel some of the crew were busying themselves getting ready for the tow whilst others were being ordered aloft so that the topsails could give a little help in the towing process. All the passengers lined the ship's side to see what was going on. Children were told to be quiet. The parents looked on with awe at the skill of the crew members who always seemed to know exactly what they were required to do, whether on deck or high above with their bare feet seeming to fasten them to the ropes and lines up there whilst their hands were busy undoing knots and pulling at canvas. Eventually the tow rope to the tug became taut as the slack was taken up and at first slightly, just very slightly, there was a feeling of forward motion accompanied by the mildest perception of a roll. Slight it might be, but it was enough for a woman of about forty years of age and who was just along from Sophie at the rail side. With one sudden great big belch she threw up, unfortunately disgorging herself upon the heads of a couple of boatmen below who five minutes before had been endeavouring to sell oranges to the departing passengers. The trading had been by way of exchanging the odd penny dropped down to them and in return they would throw back the fruit. It was remarkable how often there was much greater skill in catching the coins in the little rowboat than there was in the oranges landing on the deck! Many seemed to fall back onto the tiny vessel below to the accompaniment of curses and allegations that all was not honest. So the covering of vomit they received from the poor lady was greeted by all on board with a mixture of laughter and cheers from those at the ship's rail.

For some standing there and seeing the city that still contained their families and friends it was a scene from which they could not tear away their eyes. For others, especially the children, there was exploring to do and for some even the opportunity to visit the "heads" and relieve themselves without having to wait in an interminable queue in the way they had found necessary the previous evening when first on board. Whilst some gazed at the Liverpool shore, now almost flat countryside with only a handful of low buildings at the water's edge, others watched the opposite Cheshire shore. That side the land came to an end much sooner with a fort and a lighthouse marking its final edge. Way off in the early dusk the high mountains of Wales were silhouetted against a setting red sun. But by then it was time for the final meal of the day, at least for those ever-diminishing numbers who still felt like eating, as the ship moved further and further out into Liverpool Bay, still guided by her tug.

Next morning the four young folk were up early and made their ablutions before breakfast. Little George had found it difficult at first to get to sleep the previous evening but once his tiny eyes had closed Caroline herself had settled down without difficulty. Then again they were at the ship's side, for the motion had stopped and the tug was about to say its farewells. A small boat from their own vessel had been lowered into the water and the Master was bidding adieu to the ship's agent and the representatives of the owners. The pilot was also leaving; he was to be rowed over to the pilot boat standing patiently nearby in anticipation of returning to the shore. It was a lovely picture to behold. The pilot boat had her sail furled as she drifted gently in the breeze. Beyond her could be seen the island of Anglesey, flat save for one low hill and which was completely dwarfed by the grandeur of the mountains of the Welsh Snowdonian range that they had distantly espied before bed last night. A final wave from the Captain of the "Carthage", a modest but polite dipping of flags exchanged between the tug and her erstwhile charge, and there was a tremendous noise aloft as the sails dropped down into place and they were off. Off to America and a new life.

In the "saloon" the single steward laid out the table for breakfast for the eighteen passengers who were travelling in comparative luxury but down in the steerage class it was another matter. Nat had been appointed "captain of the mess" and which meant that he was responsible for the first week in organising the obtaining of their food rations from the purser and ensuring their table of twelve was swept and all crockery clean after each meal. One of his first duties was to obtain the hot water from the cook and to carry it along the swaying deck and then down below so that porridge could be made and tea brewed.

One of the two other families in their mess were the McNeills from the Borders of Scotland. Mr McNeill had been a shepherd caring for a large flock of sheep producing wool to supply the mills in towns such as Hawick and Jedburgh that lay amongst the rolling hills half way between Edinburgh and the northern-most parts of England. Mrs McNeill was still nursing her eighth child, a little boy of two months and the obvious apple in the eye of his seven older sisters.

The other family were from Ireland – the O'Sullivans. They had sailed first from Cork in the south of that perpetually unhappy island to Liverpool to find a passage. They had no children. Mrs O'Sullivan was a big woman who carried all before her. Maybe it was the lack of a young generation of O'Sullivans to divert her attention but Mrs O'Sullivan had cultivated a biting tongue. By contrast her husband was a mouse of a man. Not the sort of mouse that would send anyone shrieking with fear and seeking to climb onto the nearest chair but rather the sort of dormouse creature that called forth sympathy at his predicament. At least the other three men in the mess felt for him and McNeill was forever goading him on to stand up to his wife, something that was beyond the apparent capability of the poor man. In the short time they had already been on board the "Carthage" the three other men had already decided amongst themselves that the following week O'Sullivan would replace Nat as mess captain so that the wretched man could at least get away from his wife for brief moments when in line waiting for the cook to dispense his not-over-generous rations.

It was soon after breakfast that Caroline began to feel queasy and had to make a dash for the side of the ship. The wind in the Irish Sea had stiffened and there was a considerable swell running. White tops were on almost every wave and the "Carthage" was dipping and rising as each one approached. The men in the party were made of sterner stuff and found a good pipe of tobacco helped them concentrate on their conversation as to whether it really had been a good harvest last summer back home. Robert thought it had been, judging by the number of horse-shoes he had had to replace at the smithy, but Nat, always the more commercial-minded, was not so sure. A lot of the wheat had been layed by that storm a couple of weeks back; and he also knew farmers who said the milk yield was not so good due to the earlier heat that on the other hand had helped to ripen the corn. But then that was farmers all over; if one sort of weather was good for them then it was bad for the next farmer down the road. There was no satisfying all of them and many a time Robert had bit his tongue in frustration when he had heard a farmer complain one minute only to find the next that he had been able to afford a new cart, or had bought an extra few cattle to expand his herd.

Day by day as the ship made its steady progress across the Atlantic their shipboard life became routine. Some days the weather was calm and few amongst them suffered from sickness; but there were days, and especially nights, when the dark clouds hid the moon and stars. Times when the wind bore down upon them with fury and the captain would need to take down his canvas and rely on the natural momentum of winds and seas to make progress towards their ultimate destination.

Some mornings when the log was paid out to measure their advances and when a glimpse of the sun between the heavy clouds enabled the sextant to be used and the position calculated, it was found they had actually gone backward a few dozen miles.

Those nights, and even through those days, many lay in their bunks retching into tin chamber-pots and imploring the Lord to bring peace and calm to the elements. Maybe He considered it was His duty to punish the wicked on board; for many a time their pleas were ignored as the ship rolled and plunged like a corkscrew before rising up to master the next Atlantic roller. One terrifying night that reached well into the following day they were all told that no one must go on deck. Chamber pots were full to overflowing, bedding got soaked from the water that cascaded down below from the decks above, and many felt their lives were about to end amongst the fishes and other sea-creatures that were all around them. Yet at midday the order came for all appear on deck for fresh air; for the bedding to be brought up and be strung out on the line of ropes the crew had arranged. The hatches were to be opened so that the warmth of the newly-appeared sun and the wind that had veered round to the south could both dry all clothing and linen and indeed enter the bones that had shivered in wretchedness for the past eighteen hours. The fire was re-lit in the galley and a broth was served that warmed all parts of the body to the benefit of mankind in general.

One evening as the two men stood at the side of the ship smoking Robert raised with his brother-in-law what they should do once they landed. Rumour had it that another two days might see them within sight of land. They had seen icebergs in the distance the day before and one of the crew had told them that was a sure sign that land was not far off.

Before leaving they had agreed not to make the long overland journey to the new gold fields of California but rather to seek their fortunes in the area to the north of New York – funny how they called it "New England". But the question was should they first of all seek work in New York itself; indeed for example what sort of work could a blacksmith find in a big city? And could their wives find work? Sophie was a good seamstress but Caroline was more of a disposition to work in a kitchen or in domestic service, perhaps at the table. Her pregnancy was also a factor to take into account as was what to do with George whilst she was at work? There were supposed to be big houses in the city and maybe they would need staff? They must wait and see. Then where would they stay - and for how long? It was said that winters in New York could be mightily cold and travel beyond the city nigh on impossible. Should they stay in town until the spring then head north for a more settled life in some town rather like the ones they had left behind in Old England? There was much to think about, and to talk about, before they turned-in that night. Then once they had taken their decisions the two men would have to inform their wives. It was, after all, a joint venture for each couple; but it was a man's job in life to take the decisions and each was confident that his spouse would accept it without demur.

One Tuesday they sighted some fishing smacks. Fishing for cod they were told, for they were off the "Grand Banks" and somewhere beyond the horizon lay Canada and its people who had stayed loyal to the Crown when America had decided to break away some eighty years ago. The next morning they had their first real sight of land and all day they hugged it as it lay to their starboard side. Ships now appeared all over the place. Small vessels with a handful of men seeking their fortunes from the fish that lay beneath, and larger ones that seemed to be entering or departing from a myriad of rivers and ports that dotted the coast of New England. They even saw a couple of paddle streamers that were plying up and down carrying passengers between the main towns along the coast and even as far south as New York.

'Paddle steamers belonging to the Fall River Line,' the mate said they were, adding that they travelled up and down that coast every day, even in thick fogs and in winter.

It was with great interest that they even saw a big steamship coming out of the port of Boston. Wasn't that the place where all the trouble had started in their grandfathers' time? And all over a cargo of tea!

Hour by hour the "Carthage" continued her plodding southwards along the coasts of Massachusetts and Connecticut. As the sun set behind the coast of their new land, the lighthouses started to blink their warnings. "Cape Ann", that one was somewhere north of Boston, "Stonington", one of the destinations of those paddle steamers, and a number of others with odd-sounding names such as "Montauk". All blinked out their message. "Here we are. Here is the United States. Welcome, but take care!"

That night their captain put out to sea rather than enter New York as the night fell. As Wednesday dawned there seem much bustling about on deck long before the first bleary eyes of the steerage passengers were rubbed and the first toes felt for the floor. Carefully avoiding the low headroom above, the initial bodies swung out into a sitting position, breeches were pulled up over night-shirts and their occupants made off to the "heads". Those that were up early enough could see the lengthy and flat outline of Long Island reflected in the morning sun; whilst those still abed could feel the slackening of the ship in the water as she hove to, awaiting the arrival of the pilot vessel.

Soon thereafter a paddle-tug approached them and they were under tow. Gradually for the first time in weeks they turned north-about and headed through the narrow straits into Upper New York Bay. There seemed to be a number of islands through which the tug and their own pilot gently nursed them until they swung slightly to the right and entered the East River to finally tie up at one of the many piers that lay at the south-eastern corner of Manhattan Island.

At long last this stage of their journey was over, and as they descended the gangway onto the pier they once more started to feel something immovable under their feet. It was wonderful once again to be on solid earth. At first they felt a little unsteady, yet they looked forward to being able to get away from the density of humanity-packed-alongside-humanity, such as they had experienced both above and especially below decks ever since they had left Liverpool.

What they had not expected was almost the same density of humanity was to be found in New York. If Liverpool had been a busy city and port then New York was a true cauldron of activity. But they were safely there and that was what mattered. As each man, woman and child set foot on their new homeland, individual prayers of thanks were sent up to He who had guided them over the waves.

CHAPTER V

New York City, Winter 1854-55

As the two families first set foot on American soil they immediately became aware of the differences to back home in England. New York was not simply another Liverpool, it was something totally different and this became apparent at once.

When they walked around the contrast was quite evident. In Liverpool, despite the hordes of folk who would sell you an orange, carry your bags for you or even go and buy a new bonnet for you, there had been an undercurrent of organisation and discipline. But here in New York there was much more bustle and a feeling that each person was on their own, working for themselves. Thus the pace of activity – and hopefully the level of profit – was greater. Nat at once took a liking to the city but Robert was not so sure. He was more used to the measured pace of the countryman and had always found towns a bit too hectic for him. Even the old English towns that he used to go to on a market day had always been a bit too much for him.

One man who came up to them with a barrow offering to take their bags to their lodgings was a black fellow. He suddenly appeared at Caroline's elbow and when on hearing his voice she turned she got quite a fright. A tall smiling face with gleaming white teeth – at least the few that he had left were gleaming – lay behind the voice. The man was most courteous but Robert was not yet sure how to react to all the noise and activity about them; so was not yet ready to spend money on seeking help. Would they be charged a fair price? Or would they be done out of some of the precious money that they had brought with them? It was little enough in any case and they would need to find some employment pretty soon.

The range of people milling all around and the mixture of tongues was unbelievable. Liverpool, before they had left, had been bad enough but this city was beyond comprehension. As well as black and white peoples there were China-men and even quite frequently very fine-looking tall brown-skinned folk who someone told them were the original natives of the country and were called "Red Indians". They had their hair tied up in a bun at the back rather as did Caroline and Sophie. But these were men. They had heard from their parents of stories of Red Indians, but they thought they all had large rows of feathers on their heads! Maybe these were from a different tribe or they had changed head-styles when in a big city?

Before they had left the ship the little groups in their individual "messes" had each wished one another well in their new adventures. Now all that was over and Sophie and Nat, Caroline and Robert, were on their own in a strange, very strange, city and in a new land many thousands of miles away from their own dear families and the country they knew so well.

The first thing they must do was to find rooms for that night and the next few ahead. As they had landed they had been greeted by a number of men handing out leaflets advertising boarding-houses. Many offered "favorable rates" – how funny to see this spelling – whilst others were close to the ferry terminal to New Jersey which lay on the opposite bank of the Hudson River. The Hudson was much wider than the old Mersey and flowed on the opposite side of Manhattan Island to the East

River where they had landed. Other leaflets promoted their boarding houses as being convenient for "Pier Number 18 and vessels sailing up the Hudson River to Albany" or "Close to Pier 29 for those seeking onward transport to Newburgh and Poughkeepsie". Calling over a little man with a pipe stuck in the corner of his mouth and with a squint in his left eye, Robert showed him some of the leaflets and asked him which area they should go to in order to be away from the immediate vicinity of the docks where they had landed? He reckoned the prices might not be quite so high, and the comforts a little more accommodating, if they could get away from the places most popular with arriving immigrants. "Squinty", as they called him between themselves, could not read but when the names were read out to him he at once suggested somewhere over near the Hudson River the other side of Manhattan and about half an hour's walk away from where they had landed. They had to trust someone and so giving the man a coin for pushing his barrow with their trunks and cases they set off following him to the address on one of the leaflets.

The woman who opened the door in reply to their knocking was a big matronly type with a kind smile on her face. Caroline and Sophie took to her at once and she welcomed the weary travellers in and showed them two small rooms on the second floor. There was a tap at the end of the corridor and each room contained a bucket behind a screen for their private ablutions. This was collected each morning by a young girl who replaced it with a clean empty one. Mrs O'Connelly did not serve food to her guests but explained that they could get a good cheap meal around the corner at a small establishment that specialised in meals for migrants who were departing by the ferry over the

Hudson to New Jersey and whence they embarked by train to cross the country. The ferries were busiest first thing in the morning, explained their hostess, so if they waited a little while then they would often be able to get breakfast at a better price when things became quieter.

The plan worked well on their first morning. After a good breakfast of bacon and eggs – "sunny-side up" the Americans seemed to call this, a term that set the two girls off giggling with mirth – they all settled down round the table to formulate their plans for the next few days. The first thing was a job for the two men and then perhaps the girls could also obtain work. This agreed, they returned to their lodgings and the men left their womenfolk in the care of Mrs O'Connelly and set off to see what work they could find. Reckoning that anywhere near the docks would mean not only hard physical work but also low pay as there seemed so many touting for jobs, they reasoned instead that they should go somewhere in the middle of the island. Old buildings seemed to be being pulled down everywhere and new ones going up in a frenzy of development. There were buildings that were four and five storeys high. Robert had never seen such tall buildings, except of course the spires of churches.

Before long they found themselves taken on by a Frenchman who appeared to be in charge of one block that was already three storeys high and still being pushed upwards into the sky. They could start next day, and the pay was not bad. Robert was to help the man who was working over a hot fire bending metal and producing all sorts of ironwork such as door handles and window fittings. It was rather like being back in his father's smithy. Nat was to take charge of a group of bricklayers who climbed the ladders and scaffolding of wood that surrounded the edifice.

Meantime back in the care of their new-found hostess and friend, the girls discussed how they could also help towards the income they would need to build up for their future ventures in New England. Mrs O'Connelly herself had arrived like them off an immigrant ship some seven years before. She had started as a washer-woman in a big house and then met Mr O'Connelly who was a footman there. He had died the previous year after being run over by a horse and cart as his widow described, 'coming home late one night the worse for wear after a drop of the hard stuff.' So she had borrowed some money from friends and rented this building from her husband's former employer and was now letting rooms out to those who had landed like her from a ship and with nowhere to sleep.

Throughout the last few weeks of that fall and the subsequent winter of 1854-55 the two young women worked for Mrs O'Connelly's old employer. Each morning they set off early to walk to the house on Cedar Street where the Harrison family lived in some style. Mr Harrison was a partner in a shipping line that traded with South America whilst his good lady seemed to spend most of her time producing heirs for the family fortune and which would have to be shared amongst six boys and five girls, ranging from William aged 15 down to the eight-month old baby Lucilla. All this provided more than enough work for Sophie, acting as seamstress in a small room at the top of the house. Caroline meantime was a parlor-maid and carried out such duties as she was directed by the butler, a tall man with white hair and who always wore gloves to match. He had been a footman with Mr Harrison's family in Virginia before the family business moved to New York as trade with Brazil had increased. Pay was not good, but the two English women were both loyal to their employer and worked hard to keep their posts. Week by week, and month by month, they were able to put a little aside after paying Mrs O'Connelly for the rent. For the cost of an extra penny a day she also kept little George beside her when his mother was at work.

At the same time Robert and Nat carried on working for the Frenchman. He seemed to have quite a few sites that he was involved with and the husbands always enjoyed it when they were sent to a new one in Manhattan. Sometimes they were at the same locations and at others they were apart but they occasionally managed to meet up for a beer before going home in the evening. They particularly enjoyed the opportunity to see the sights and all that was going on in the waters that surrounded the island. Indeed that was the real advantage as far as they were concerned of being in New York. When they had first approached the city on the old "Carthage" it had looked as if New York was a city dominated by churches for the many spires had stood out high on the skyline. Now they were getting to know it well they had come to realise that docks and shipping, commercial buildings and trade, were more part of the Manhattan scenery than churches. Both rivers, the Hudson to the west and the East whose name spoke for itself, were lined by piers. Each pier had a number and if you were going south to Philadelphia you went to Pier 12 on the banks of the Hudson but for New Orleans it was Pier 15 and for Charleston Pier 20. Over on the shore of the East River anyone arriving from Liverpool by the Black Ball Line would first step onto

American soil at Pier 23, whereas the "Liverpool Line" itself tied up at Pier 16 at Coffee House Slip at the end of a street with the curious name of "Wall Street".

Beyond these individual piers, with destinations to all over the world, the banks of the East River were dotted with shipyards right up to 11th Street. Early each morning crowds of workers crossed over from Brooklyn on the opposite bank in a continual stream of paddle ferries that reached the island of Manhattan as far up as the Williamsburg Ferry at the end of Grand Street. On a fine morning it was fun from one of the building sites for Nat and Robert to watch these little ships dodge in and out between the larger vessels not just from foreign lands but also those that were plying their passenger trades along the coast of New England. Those long-distance ferries from Hartford and New Haven were destined for Pier 23. In the true spirit of American competition, some from Providence in Rhode Island had also stopped to pick up travellers from New Haven and were offering to land them by the Fulton market. When they first saw this early morning river traffic Robert wondered what would happen when there was fog on the river or a blinding snowstorm coming out of the north. The lookouts at the bows would have to have sharp eyes in their heads.

And so the "fall" – they were beginning to use that term instead of "autumn" that they had used in England – turned into winter and for three long weeks the men were laid off and had no building work as snow lay thick on the ground.

Then true to nature the days once more started to lengthen and in the spring of 1855 life returned to the building trade in Manhattan as people began to feel the winter in their bones alleviated by the first rays of warm sunshine. Men were now more inclined to tip their hats to the ladies in the street and the collars of their fur coats – on those who could afford fur coats – were turned down and ears once more exposed to the air around them.

All the while Caroline continued her duties at the tea table in Cedar Street but shortly before Easter her kind employer agreed that she should stop until the baby was born, adding that her place would be kept for her if she wanted to return. A week later, early one morning as the sun was rising over the East River and filtering its rays in between the tall buildings that were fast becoming a feature of Manhattan, the Jackson family had its first American-born addition. Mrs O'Connolly and a neighbour down the passage helped to deliver Ellen Jackson and introduce her to her mother.

In the men's world meantime, employers began to look for workers and in the construction trade the wooden scaffolding that had survived the winter snows and gales was checked as secure and construction re-commenced where it had been left-off the previous fall. Those new half-finished buildings seemed from afar to be once more covered by ant-like creatures climbing over them as they rose to the dizzy heights of six and even seven floors.

By early April Robert and Nat were again earning good money in the employ of "Monsieur" Dubois. The Frenchman insisted on everyone addressing him in the old style of the country from where he had come after the French Emperor Napoleon, under whom he had fought in his youth, had been defeated by the English at the Battle of Waterloo in 1815.

Despite the good money that they were once again earning now spring had arrived, the months of unemployment when the rent had had to be found from the meagre wages of their wives had left a nasty taste in the mouths of Robert and Nat. Back in England in the old days it had always been a man's job to earn the money for the family and weather seldom interfered that way. Here in New York it was very different. The winters were both much longer and much colder. The only money the two young husbands had managed to earn was to team up with a couple of other recent immigrants – an Italian and a Russian – and between them all act as shovellers pushing the snow away from the steps and sidewalks around the homes of the wealthy after it had swept down deep into the centre of the city, driven by bitter northerly winds. They had supplemented this income, which relied so much on the unpredictable weather, by chopping up wood and stoking the furnaces in the same homes. Both early in the morning, and then again at night, they had to ensure the fires would keep going; especially until their early morning visit again next day.

The prospect of hot summers, working all day helping to construct new houses and tall offices even with good pay but followed by the uncertain winters, was beginning to make the two brothers-in-law restless. Frequently when working on a high building they would be distracted by the ships' sirens down on the East River. The regular-as-clockwork morning arrival at 7 am of the Fall Line overnight steamer from Providence, and of others from Boston and the various Connecticut ports such as New Haven and Hartford, was almost part of their routine. One particular ship – or its sister vessel – always arrived just as the men were having their first meal break from the heavy work of climbing up the various ladders attached to the wooden scaffolding with a hod of bricks on their shoulders. As each building rose from second to third to fourth floor and beyond the climb got more wearisome and never quite managed to compensate for the extra view.

It was one such morning when high up on the scaffolding, and whilst eating their bread and cheese and gazing down at the river below full of little ferries crossing to and fro between Manhattan Island and Brooklyn, ferries which were dodging the overnight paddle steamships arriving from Connecticut and Rhode Island, that Robert remarked that perhaps it was time for the two families to move on and try their luck further up in New England. That had always been their plan and perhaps now was the time to act.

Before more than a few weeks had passed it was one warm June evening that witnessed both families finally prepared to say farewell to New York City and setting off for a new life further east in Rhode Island.

Had they been still living in England they would, by the mid 1850s, have expected to make their journey to their new home by train as much of England by that period was already criss-crossed by a network of tracks owned by different railway companies. But in the north eastern United States the Hudson River was still an insuperable obstruction to the building of a railway from the island that was New York, to Boston. Moreover the many rivers flowing down to the seaboard of the Connecticut coast meant that so many bridges would need to be built over them that at least for now one could only reach Boston by first sailing to New Haven and then taking the long journey inland to Hartford and back once more down to the coast and so on to Providence before finally arriving at Boston. To avoid all this laborious and tiring journey most folk used the coastal steamships that plied up and down the coast day and night.

Pre-eminent amongst the shipping companies was the Fall River Line with its vessels such as the "State of Maine" and the "Metropolis". It was on their sister ship – the "Empire State" – that Robert and Caroline with George and Ellen, together with Nat and Sophie, embarked one evening.

They had taken their belongings down to the agents that morning. All their worldly goods looked somewhat pathetic as they saw them piled up and fastened with ropes onto the wagon as it left for the pier. Once more they were to spend a night at sea and again it was to start a new life in a new unknown land.

The "Empire State" was an exciting ship on which to be travelling. She was over three hundred feet long with two big side-paddles. Each paddle lay behind a large boiler with its tall black funnel in front of it. There was plenty of open deck-space and she had her name emblazoned in large letters immediately below the paddle guards. Already it was said that any voyage on the "Empire State" could be exciting – excitement perhaps tinged with a little touch of trepidation. She had been built in 1847 and only two years later she was part-burned down to the water-line in a terrible fire. Such fires of course were not uncommon with the timber-built vessels of the period. Although they were not to know it at the time of their own journey from New York it was only a matter of weeks later that the "Empire State" was to hit a rock in thick fog whilst sailing back to New York. On that occasion she again partially sank but was raised after a few days and repaired only to suffer a boiler explosion weeks later which killed three crew members although fortunately the 225 passengers all survived. But all that lay in the future for this beautiful ship.

As soon as the women had found their berths they joined their men-folk on the side-rail watching the more wealthy passengers arriving in their horse-drawn cabs. Some men were obviously coming straight from business for their associates had accompanied them to the pier. Others came aboard holding little but their carpet-bags. Perhaps some of these were salesmen from the many textile mills in Rhode Island and Massachusetts and who had been showing their factories' wares to merchants in New York City. There was much doffing of those tall black "stove-pipe" hats to each other as these gentlefolk headed for their overnight cabins or for the smoking saloon. One tall man with a monocle in his right eye caught the attention of Caroline. She nudged Sophie and murmured under her breath that she was sure the young woman on his arm was not his wife and that he was taking the opportunity of a little extra comfort on the overnight sail.

As the hands on the clock on the pier office moved to the hour the general clatter of the dockside and the chatter of the passengers at the ships rails was dominated by a strong bellow from the ship's siren and the air was filled with small flecks of black soot coming from the dark smoke that emanated from the two funnels. With shouts from both the crew and the dock workers on the pier the ropes were taken off the bollards and dropped into the water before being hauled onto the ship. A shudder went through the vessel as first one and then the second side-paddle started to slowly turn, churning up the dark fast-flowing waters as she backed out. There was a further loud ringing of bells as the Captain ordered the engines to slow down to allow a larger steamer, packed with incoming immigrants, to pass by.

That vessel, fresh from her Atlantic crossing, had a list to her starboard side for her decks were crowded with the newcomers getting their first glimpse of their future homeland. The British flag flapped in the evening air from the stern of the larger ship and the sight of it sent a flutter through the hearts of both Robert and Caroline. A couple of weeks ago the folk on the other vessel might have been living not far from their own parents back in beloved Cheshire. Maybe they even knew them and could have had some news of the families back "home". But Robert and Caroline would no longer be in New York City to hear that news. This was one of the great characteristics of the USA. People were constantly on the move. Some arrived, some departed. Between them they were all helping each other to create a new land of opportunity and now Robert, Caroline, Ned and Sophie were all off to make their next contribution away in upper New England.

Soon the "Empire State" was starting to pick up speed as she headed along the East River, keeping the island of Manhattan on her left or larboard side. On this part of the island cows were still grazing and there were trees reaching down to the water's edge. Soon they were through Hell Gate and the water became a little more choppy. It was time for the ladies to turn in, whilst the two men gazed back along the twin white wakes created by the big paddles at the last of the twinkling lights of New York City.

74

CHAPTER VI

Off to New England

Gazing back at the now becoming ever-more far-off lights of New York as they started to fade into the distance, the two brothers-in-law each had their own private thoughts. The day had been a long one. From early dawn the two families had been up quickly stowing their overnight clothes and the remnants of the items that were not already in the trunks and packing cases that stood in the lobby. Then there had been the farewells to Mrs O'Connelly their landlady and to the families next door on both sides. Part way through the morning various other friends with whom they had become acquainted whilst in New York had called into say good-bye. But then they had to be off. The carrier had called, and all their belongings to start them off in yet another new life were stacked up on the cart. So much was there on the vehicle that Caroline felt sorry for the half-starved horse, "nag" she called it in her old English terminology, that she doubted if it could haul the load down to the pier.

As soon as it had departed they set off themselves on foot for the ship. So often when in the past Robert and George had been high up on some building site and the working day was coming to a close, they had seen that little procession of ships sail out of their different piers on the Hudson and, rounding Battery Point, head up the East River. From about three o'clock onwards and usually as punctual as the old grandfather clock in the kitchen back in England, the first of the coastal steamers would set off. They had all left by around five in the early evening for New Haven, Hartford, New London and as far away as Stonington, Providence, and even Fall River, their massive side-paddles thrashing the waters of first the Hudson and then the East Rivers six nights a week. The fleet was a beautiful scene.

And so it was to be one early June afternoon in 1856, as the two families gathered at the pier-side and waited their turn to go on board. In some ways it was a pity that they could not go by train because of those large rivers and instead had to make use of the network of steamship companies that had grown up during the last thirty years.

Most of these lines operated between New York and one individual port but the number of lines, the destinations and even the very ships themselves, seemed to vary from season to season. Many operated throughout the winter as well as in summer, but whilst during the summer months they were mostly crowded with wealthy folk escaping the heat of the city, during the rest of the year the decks were filled with ordinary folk going about their daily commercial and family travels. The boats carried freight as much as they carried passengers. Indeed at times there was so much freight stacked on the decks on board that it was almost impossible to find room for a quiet smoke. In any case smoking had to be done with care. Much of the east-bound cargo was comprised of bales of cotton that had come up from the southern states and which were heading for the mills of eastern Connecticut, for Rhode Island and for Massachusetts – especially around Fall River. In the early New York mornings the returning overnight boats could be seen unloading everything from finished cloth and cotton goods to the wide range of industrial and domestic products that were the efforts of the manufactories of those states.

Once their trunks were stowed safely they had gone to find their overnight accommodation. In some ways the bunks in which they were scheduled to pass the night were less comfortable than those on which they had crossed the Atlantic a couple or so years back. However it was only for one night and then they would have to find somewhere more accommodating once they were ashore.

As the clock hands had reached the appointed time there was a flurry of activity and the blast of the ship's siren told all, both on board the ships and for miles around, even as far as the distant New Jersey shore line the other side of the river, that they were off. Plumes of smoke poured up into the heavens from the two black smoke stacks that were on either side of the vessel and adjacent to the boilers and the paddles that they drove. Slowly she had backed out into the Hudson and turned her nose south in order to round the southern tip of the island of Manhattan. Ahead another steamer, bound for Hartford, far up the Connecticut River, was doing the same. Another was swinging into line behind their own. All these captains were obviously well-practised in their chosen profession and they each knew their place in the overnight order of travel. Soon they were turning past Battery Point and with Staten Island over to their right they were heading into the East River. Shipyards lay to their left on the Manhattan shore. Many of these great big wooden steamers such as the "Empire State" on which they were travelling that evening had been built in New York at those yards and on those slip-ways. Timber was floated down the Hudson from upstate New York or down the Atlantic coast from Maine and Massachusetts for the yards. Of course ships made of iron had started to appear in New York but iron was heavy and expensive so not for the bread-and-butter trade of the New England coastal steamers of the 1850s.

The "Great Britain" built by that English genius Isambard Kingdom Brunel, and which they had seen in Liverpool before they had sailed for America, was made of iron. Indeed she had at one time been sailing between Liverpool and New York but was now taking migrants to Australia. Iron was alright for big trans-Atlantic ships but overnight steamers carrying cotton, commercial travellers and holiday makers could never be built of iron.

Steadily and majestically, as the sun began to set behind them, the little flotilla of night-ships had made their way through the churning waters of Hell Gate and passing close to Rikers Island headed for the Sound. There were six ships in all that evening and it was a very pretty sight to see.

After they had finished the meal that they had brought with them in a large basket, and the men had each had a couple of bottles of beer, the two women and the children had now turned in. The men had repaired to the starboard side and idly looked towards the low-lying coast of Long Island as they smoked their cigars. The rays of the setting sun behind their backs were picking out the small farmhouses on the shoreline and they could see cattle grazing down to the water's edge.

Little groups of men were to be seen all over the decks. Some had settled down on bales or crates and were playing cards, others were mumbling in low voices that sometimes changed into bellows of raucous laughter, doubtless the result of some joke or anecdote of a dubious nature. Gradually the level of chatter to be heard on the deck lowered as in twos and threes the men drifted off to go to sleep. The wealthier amongst them retired to their state rooms, beneath the gaps in the doors through which a few lamps could already be seen to be burning as those gentlemen's companions-of-the-night awaited them.

Robert and Nat were in no mood yet for bed. They were not making a regular voyage that they had to repeat commercially on a frequent basis nor were they on vacation. For them travelling up the coast of Connecticut was another major step in their lives and uncertainty lay ahead both for them and for their families. The two men wanted to enjoy every minute of this adventure. They had looked round the vessel and as they had done so Robert had espied a small metal plate that had been put up by the shipyard when the "Empire State" had been built in 1848. The shipyard where she had been constructed was Samuel Sneeden of New York. She was a massive 1,691 tons gross and 305 feet long. The ship was over 40 feet wide and was shown to have a depth of 13 feet. It had cost the Fall Line company 200,000 dollars to have her built and then only a year later they had had to spend half as much again due to a fire that had destroyed a large amount of her superstructure of cabins and saloons.

But tonight was not a time to dwell on things like that. It was a night – and a journey – of adventure. They had given up good jobs in the building trade and had little but their natural energy that went with their age, and their knowledge of the construction industry, to give them the advantage over others that living in the United States of to-day seemed to need.

Fortunately they could both read – as could their wives for they had been at the same "dame school" back in England. They could read, they could write, and they had mastered the puzzles of arithmetic that had been so useful in getting their jobs in Manhattan. But where did the future call them?

The ship's bell sounded and at long last the two of them decided to call it a day and get some sleep. Goodness knows where they would next put down their heads. As they walked past the great big paddle and felt the heat from the boiler in front of it, they passed a couple of men who were jabbering away in a foreign lingo. "Frenchies" thought Robert, as they squeezed past between the side of the superstructure that contained a cabin or saloon and the men who were leaning over the rails. The men were peering into the dark and one was gesticulating to the accompaniment of a high pitched voice. He turned to Nat.

'M'sieu,' he grabbed Nat's arm and pointed ahead of them.

Robert and Nat both looked in the direction of the outstretched arm with its long effeminate Gallic finger at the furthest point. He could see the sparkle of the white wash created by the paddles of the ship in front – the New Haven bound steamer – but the Frenchman was pointing beyond that, to a vessel yet further ahead in the little procession. One could see in the darkness the glow of the two boiler fires. Yet the more they stared into the night the more they began to understand the cause of the excitement. The glow was too large for the quick glimpse that was afforded when the firebox on a ship's boiler was opened for more wood to be thrown in and was then quickly closed again to create the draught in order for the fire to heat the boilers. This seemed to be a larger fire and the flames seemed to be reaching higher than the superstructure. Across the dark waters of Long Island Sound the urgent sound of ships' bells was carried by the night wind that blew from the Atlantic that lay ahead. The bells from the two vessels were sounding the alarm. That ship was on fire!

By now the two Frenchmen and their English fellow travellers had been joined by half a dozen other men leaning over the ship's railing and pointing at the frightening scene that lay a couple of miles or so ahead of them. On their own ship there was the sudden running of feet as members of the crew turned out and went to their stations. Under them they could feel a quickening of pace as their paddles seems to start turning faster as the master urged his ship forward to the rescue.

Soon the deck was crowded with folk who had been raised from their slumbers by the bell of their own vessel sounding a warning. Their own wives, with the children covered by blankets in their arms, worked their way through the mêlée to join them as the ship started to heel over on one side with so many folk all crowding on the deck for the best vantage point. Indeed the tilt became so considerable that the paddle on the opposite side was starting to thrash the air rather than the water and the captain needed to steer her with considerable skill to enable him to keep straight ahead.

After what seemed a long time, but was in fact a short period, they came abreast of the stricken steamer. By now she was well alight and the crew could be seen throwing the bales of cotton overboard to prevent the fire spreading further. The trouble was that many of those bales were already alight themselves and were becoming a frightening hazard as they bobbed about in the dark sea and started to float towards the other ships that were coming to the rescue. The night was penetrated by screams of fear, especially from the women and children over there. Some were jumping into the murky black water to escape the inferno that was now raging. Some were clinging to bales that were not alight, or to pieces of deck-furniture or wooden crates, or in fact anything that would float. A few could find nothing, or could not swim, and were being taken by the waters further and further away from the stricken vessel and its rescuing compatriots. Occasionally the screams would rise to a crescendo and then suddenly stop as their owners sank down into the depths; and the hopes of a child for its future or the commercial dreams of a father of four, would come to a bitter end amongst the cold engulfing arms of Long Island Sound.

The captain of their ship was in a dilemma. The camaraderie of the sea demanded that he help his opposite number, its crew and the remaining passengers to the best of his ability. Yet he must always remember that his own ship was constructed of wood and that it only needed a spark, if he drew too close, to land on one of his own bales of cotton and there would be two not one emergencies in the Sound that night.

Having manoeuvred as close as safety permitted the two big paddle wheels were stopped and their vessel lay motionless in the water, save for the lapping from the slight swell of the waves on the ship's hull. Crew and male passengers alike threw ropes over the side for any swimmer who could grasp them and be hauled to safety. The womenfolk meantime kept searching with their tear-stained eyes at the dark waters for the tell-tale splash or cry of help from someone in distress. Logs of timber, destined for the furnaces, were jettisoned over the side in the hope that perhaps they might be grabbed by anxious hands and someone kept afloat until help could reach them.

Caroline and Sophie joined the other women in their efforts to spot people in the water. Sometimes they would think they saw someone swimming towards them, other times they could see the whole scene quite clearly when flames suddenly shot up from the burning vessel and illuminated the ghastly picture that lay before them. Most distressing of all was when a hand was raised into the night sky followed by an ear-piercing scream before the waters closed over the poor soul.

Twice Caroline burst into tears at the sight of motionless children's bodies floating past the side of their ship. The first was a girl of about thirteen with a tartan coat over her night-dress and the long plaits of her hair trailing in the gentle swell. The other was a boy who could not have been more than eight years old. Doubtless the night before he would have been full of excitement at the prospect of sailing on a big ship with his parents. On going on board he would have explored every nook and cranny before succumbing to his mother's instructions to retire to bed as "there would be a busy day ahead". Never again would that young lad – and who perhaps had been destined to play a great or small part in the future of the United States – see the dawn break on New England's shores. As Caroline sobbed at the scene Sophie put a gentle arm round her sister-in-law and called Robert over to comfort his distraught wife.

After two hours the fires had dwindled down to a few flickers about a burned-out hull and the rest of the flotilla started to gently move away as each captain in turn decided his own vessel could do no more. Somehow Robert and the others, men, women and children, could not tear themselves away from the side of the ship as the wheels started to turn. Turn ever so slowly at first, as if the Captain was afraid that the big paddles might pick up some body and fling it into the air before plunging it down into those waters below for a final farewell. But as the steamer moved further and further from the wreck the speed was picked up and in half an hour they had resumed their overnight journey. A journey now where few spoke, no one laughed and where next morning, having left the other coastal steamers to go their separate ways in the early dawn, they paddled up the river to the pier in a very sombre mood.

It was still cold out on the river as the passengers all stood about on the deck awaiting the gang-plank to be pulled onto the ship once the ropes were secured to the quayside. Not many had slept after the ghastly incidents of the previous evening. State-rooms that normally were reserved for one person or for a family had been requisitioned and commandeered to takes twice or thrice the usual numbers. The Ladies' Saloon had had blankets spread on the floors to give a little comfort to the female survivors and the children who huddled round their mothers' skirts; whilst in some cases the self-same mothers and others lay gazing up at the ornate white ceiling not believing that their beloved husband or child was no long with them in this world and instead had been gathered up, together with fellow passengers, into the arms of He who cared for all.

Amongst those who had managed to swim to the safety of the ship was a Baptist minister who spent the whole of the night talking to bereft parents, holding the hands of mothers whilst he prayed with them. Shortly before the ship tied up, and as the paddles were turning ever more slowly approaching the dock, that man of God held a short service. A service that was attended by every passenger on the vessel and as many of the crew as the Captain could spare from their duties. It would be the last time that those who had set off from New York the night before on this self-same coastal steamer – and those who had embarked on another vessel that now was somewhere adrift as a burnt-out hulk in Long Island Sound – would all gather together. It was as they finished the Lord's Prayer with a final 'Amen' that the first ropes were thrown to the waiting men on the dockside. No one who that night had sought comfort from the minister with his still-sodden long black coat would have guessed that within him was contained all the fear and despair of one whose own beloved wife had slipped from his grasp and sunk into her own watery grave off the coast of Connecticut.

At the quayside a special train was waiting to convey the passengers away from the scene and in the direction of Boston. Blue-coated soldiers, with the collars pulled up against the cold morning air, were in attendance to ensure an orderly disembarkation whilst local doctors, supported by many of the town's ladies, waited to help those who could not care for themselves. A series of carriages and wagons, with horses stamping impatiently as they stood in their harnesses in the cold of the early dawn, waited to carry the injured to local homes where they would be looked after until fit and ready to take up their shattered lives once more. Evidence of American hospitality and charity for those less fortunate than themselves was in abundance and could be found all around.

Caroline and Robert, together with Sophie and Nat and the children, waited patiently their turn to walk down onto the pier. Caroline cradled a small baby who someone had hastily dumped into her arms after it had been fished out of the water during the frantic scenes of the night before. The two husbands had gone round the ship later making enquiries of all and sundry to see if the parents of the little boy could be traced, but to no avail. The child was about a year old and had spent much of its time crying until exhaustion blissfully brought it sleep at about three o'clock in the morning. Caroline had removed its wet clothes and had taken off her petticoat and wrapped it round the child for warmth. Before leaving New York the previous day she had deliberately chosen a warm flannel petticoat because of being at sea. Now her choice had proven a great blessing. When the good and kindly minister had come round and spoken with them the couple had asked his advice what to do with the child. He had told her that her first duty to both the child and to God was to care for it until such time as the parents would perhaps be located.

'What do I call it?' she had asked him.

'Call him "Matthew", the first of the Apostles,' he told her, before moving on to comfort a mother and her now-fatherless seven children.

And so it was that Matthew became a member of the Jackson family. Over the next few months Robert and Caroline made numerous enquiries and even placed a Notice in the Hartford Courant in order to try and find the true parents of the little lad. No response was forthcoming and as time went on and the couple grew to love this child from the waters of Long Island Sound they found themselves less and less anxious to find any relatives and more and more disposed to take him into the bosom of their own family.

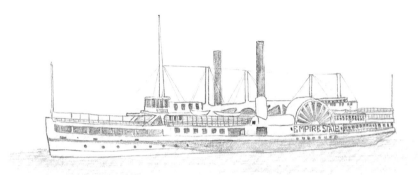

Paddle Steamer 'Empire State'
Sketch by Gill Kegel

Paddle Steamer 'Puritan' toy model
Photo by Ian Kegel

Robert himself had found employment with the local railroad company whilst his brother-in-law Nat became a supervisor at a local textile mill. Together the two families had managed to save up and purchase three acres of land from a local farmer on the edge of the town. They worked in the long evenings of the hot summer that followed their arrival constructing two houses on the plot. Their experiences in their previous jobs in Manhattan proved to be invaluable and the results were the envy of many homeowners in the community. At the rear the women raised chickens and a few pigs. Sophie worked at the local mill where her husband was the supervisor in charge of taking the bales of cloth down to the railroad for the Boston market and to the coastal vessels for shipping back to New York. Caroline herself had Matthew to care for and bring up in addition to their own children and it was she who prepared a good solid meal for all of them when they returned from mill and railroad alike in the evening.

As the years passed the two families prospered. Nat eventually became a partner in the mill whilst Robert found himself responsible for all the purchasing of supplies for the railroad company. Both families increased in numbers with Robert and Caroline having their own three girls and three boys in addition to Matthew whilst over the years Sophie and Nat had six girls and five boys. But in the secret depths of the minds of Robert and Caroline there was a very special love for that tiny child, who it seemed God had thrust into their care one night when the cold dark waters of Long Island Sound were aglow with the flames that raced into the heavens and the silent lapping sea was rent with screams as so many a hand reached up, before disappearing beneath the waves.

Robert and Caroline never spoke to Matthew of that terrible night and of his unknown origins. They saw no sense to disturb the happy childhood with which he was blessed in their care. As time passed he grew up to be the natural leader of the little pack of siblings and cousins who chased each other around the two houses, down to the cellars and up into the attics when it was wet or the house lay under the months of New England snow. In summer they built their own tents and houses in the two gardens and would sometimes go off to the local farm and help with the harvest, piling the sheaves of wheat in rows of stooks to dry before threshing. When the summer holidays were over the older children would return to school, for their parents always insisted that writing and arithmetic were essential if they were to succeed. At home the mothers also taught them history and geography; and of how three thousand miles away they had grandparents back in England.

In the September of each year Matthew, as leader of the little army, would march them out on Saturdays through the forests that surrounded the town so that they could see the beautiful colours of the fall. He knew the names of the different types of maple and would sit them in a circle and test them by producing a number of leaves he had picked up whilst following the paths that morning, and he would ask them to identify the species. He had also learned a few words and phrases from the local Indian tribe that lived in the area and was always proud to display his knowledge of the land by referring to this or that feature in their language.

Every Christmas two parcels would arrive from England, one for each family. Sometimes a "likeness" or small painting would be found at the bottom of the packet. As time went on these portraits depicted grandparents who seemed to be getting older and older. Then one year Robert and Caroline received nothing. December turned into January and the temperatures dropped down as the snow lay five feet deep in the gardens of the two houses. Even the coastal steamers were not plying to New York as the river was frozen and that year the ice had even closed the entry from Long Island Sound through Hell Gate into the East River. Some steamers were making their way round the ocean-side of Long Island but it was not a winter's journey to be recommended and few merchants were keen to put their cargoes at risk from an angry Atlantic storm.

It was in the fall that Robert made his big decision. Caroline had finally recognised that she would never again read those long letters from her father or mother, and that she would no longer know the latest news from the town or learn which farmer had needed an excess of shoes for his horses or if the "autumn" (as they called the fall back at home in England) had brought a good harvest.

That year, as the trees turned into their magnificent colours of vivid gold and bright red, Robert finally left his post with the railway company and set up on his own. Over the years he had built up a vast network of contacts whilst purchasing for the railway, but he had come to the conclusion that there was more money to be made supplying the transport industry then buying on its behalf. And so on the first Monday after Thanksgiving the new company of "Jackson and Sons, Suppliers to the Railroad Industry" was gazetted and a large room at the back of the house was used as the office for the fledgling company. As the two families sat round the table with their Thanksgiving turkey they toasted the new company and the approaching year of 1861 with enthusiasm. They were now all part of the American Dream and prosperity was lapping at their doors.

CHAPTER VII

Building an empire

The second half of the nineteenth century was an age of empires. Over in Europe those empires were political ones, created as smaller countries combined for different reasons into mergers with their neighbours. Sometimes these new nations were the result of friendly agreements but at other times they were only achieved by war of neighbour against neighbour. Many of these results, however obtained, frequently signified their achievements by giving the new heads of the empires the title of "Emperor". In France the nephew of the long-dead Napoleon gave himself the title of "Napoleon III" and proclaimed he was head of the "Third Empire". In Vienna Franz Joseph, the "Emperor of the Austro–Hungarian Empire", ruled from northern Italy through much of the centre of Europe and the Balkans, so that his lands bordered to the south with those of the Turkish Sultan and in the north with the mini-states that joined together to become the "German Empire" under a "Kaiser".

In Great Britain Prime Minister Benjamin Disraeli gave his own Queen Victoria the title "Empress of India". Her empire stretched around the globe from the frozen north of Canada over the vast plains of India down to the deserts of Australia and snow-clad mountains of New Zealand. All these far-flung lands were held together by a string of small colonies and outposts such as Gibraltar, Aden, Singapore and Hong Kong. British children's board games used to refer to these small dots on their maps of the British Empire as "coaling-points", so named because they were where British merchant ships and the Royal Navy would put in to stock-up with fuel as they processed to the next leg of their journeys around the world that was the "British Empire".

But the United States of America was not yet ready to play her part as a world power. First she had to unify herself and make sure her peoples – drawn as they had been from many different nations – were of one mind and one determination to be a "united states" of America. In one way that was a building of an internal empire and which needed a national political self-confidence that could only come from economic self-confidence. Later they would first show they had achieved it by taking on the fading power of one of Europe's most ancient of medieval empires, Spain. Yet first they had to win-through by uniting via a bloody civil war after which they needed to build their economic strength starting with the individual efforts of each other. "Jackson and Sons, suppliers to the Railroad Industry" were to be part of that surge of self-assurance.

It was not just the Jackson family and their cousins and all their friends who had confidence in the coming New Year of 1861. Old President Buchanan was due to step down at the White House whilst someone called Abraham Lincoln, a Republican, had been elected and so the change was to be for the good.

Because he was untried as a serious politician the new President was likely to be cautious and the country needed that stability. Yes, Mr Lincoln was opposed to the new territories in the west being allowed to accept slavery when they each joined the union in turn, but that was a problem those in Washington would have to sort out with the slave-masters in the South. And that "South" was a long way away from here in New England. Here they, Robert and Caroline together with Nat and Sophie, had proper work to do.

Rhode Island lay under its normal carpet of deep snow as Christmas turned into New Year. Progress on railway construction was slow, even some of the overnight steamer services up and down the coast were cancelled due to bad weather, but as the nights eventually started to grow shorter and the days longer the orders for supplies started to trickle in to Jackson & Sons. Robert was away from home quite often, sometimes to Hartford or New York, sometimes by rail up to Boston. He was in Hartford one April day when he read in The Courant that a small garrison of soldiers at a place called Fort Sumter had been attacked by troops loyal to the pro-slave states and had had to surrender. It was a troubled Robert who travelled back that night on the boat up east.

Little by little those squabbles down in the South seemed to be growing more ominous and the latest news from the "War" as it was now being called was starting to have an effect up in New England. There were big problems for some of the mills as their supplies of cotton from down south began to dry up. This was affecting Nat's company, but demand for supplies of a wide range of items for the railroads was increasing rapidly. And so were the profits for Jackson & Sons. More work, and Robert's frequent absences from home, meant placing a tremendous burden on Caroline so in the spring of '62 Nat resigned from his work at the mill and became a partner in the family firm.

As the impact of the Civil War began to spread far and wide the railroad industry came into great demand for moving both goods, including ammunition and troops, from one front to another. The great increase over the tracks meant more and more maintenance was needed and that in turn required supplies that had to be produced quickly. Robert and Nat soon needed extra help, but before long many of the younger men were volunteering for the army and the casualty rates started to go up and up. Conscription was introduced, so reducing further the pool of men available to the firm. So important was their work at Jackson & Sons that the company began to be recognised as a major contributor to the success of the Union's ability to support its armies. Robert travelled widely at this stage and his return home from each trip was not just eagerly awaited by Caroline and the family for personal reasons but he was also able to give them the latest news on the fighting in different parts of the country.

Two years into the war Robert took the momentous decision that for certain steel supplies for the tracks he would have to go over to England.

It was around ten years since they had sailed to New York on the old "Carthage" and of course that had been steerage class and under sail. Now he would be able to enjoy a little more luxury with his meals put before him by a steward and he would have a cabin that he need only share with one other fellow passenger. His ship would sail from Boston to Liverpool and it would fly the American flag.

The voyage itself proved uneventful and the seas were calm whilst his cabin-companion turned out to be pleasant enough. At first the captain had been fearful in case they ran into any ship from the Confederate Navy that might be roaming the Atlantic looking for Union prey. It was with a sigh of relief all round when early one morning they could see in the distance the tops of the mountains of Wales picked out by the dawn's rising sun. Before lunch was served on board in the saloon they started to pass vessels flying the English flag and shortly afterwards they were to heave-to off the island of Anglesey to await the pilot cutter so that they could be guided into the River Mersey.

As he stood at the ship's rail looking from one side of the river to the other memories of their departure for their new life in America came crowding back. What would England be like? At least she was not being torn asunder by a civil war – they had had theirs over here two hundred years ago. It must have been equally bloody and must also have seen families torn apart but time had been a great healer. Would that happen one day back in his new country? He hoped so. George was 10 years old now, Ellen was nearly nine and Matthew about eight. The latest of the family of seven had just been born. What sort of America would they all grow up in? Would any of them ever come over to England? The firm was doing well and if they all pulled together then the opportunities for a good life would be there for them to grasp.

But in the meantime he must get on and do the business in Birmingham and surrounding towns where the English steel industry was thriving – for this old nation was sending out her engineers and her steel to build railways all over the world.

Robert had arrived on a Friday in Liverpool and he was not due to go down to meet his contacts until the coming Monday. He had planned to look up their old cousins in Toxteth for the weekend. A brisk cab drive paid for in shillings and pence (how funny it was to be using that old money again) soon brought him to the door. Much to Robert's amazement the door was opened by his very own brother Joshua and it was not long before, in front of a coal fire, the news from both sides of the Atlantic was being exchanged. The long silences with no letters now started to become clear. Their father, James, had succumbed to an outbreak of cholera during a previous winter. He had never been a correspondent as he could not write and had left their mother Anne to keep the family news spreading to America. But Anne had fallen on an icy puddle some years ago and had broken her hip. She had never recovered and now both parents were at rest in that graveyard that lay in the shadow of St Werburgh's church. Young Joshua had been too inexperienced to take on the smithy so his Toxteth cousins had persuaded him to come and live with them. He was a clerk at a local bank.

The following week was a hectic one and everyone seemed keen to do business with Robert for his credit was good and he was known to encourage the loyalty of his suppliers by always paying his bills on time.

It was only later, during a weekend of his visit when he travelled around some of the Lancashire and Cheshire cotton towns in the North to look up his old family haunts, that Robert experienced a degree of hostility. Some of the mills were having to close down through lack of raw cotton from the Southern States and there seemed to be a common opinion in the north of England that the Union should have minded its own business and allowed the slave states to just run themselves as they wished.

As was only to be expected it was a sad day when Robert visited the graves of his parents. The drizzling rain was rolling off the nearby hills when he stood bareheaded just staring at the little mound of earth, below which lay so many happy memories. He must have been there, a lonely and wet figure, for some time when a kindly voice behind him asked if he needed help? Turning he found himself face to face with old Vicar Forsyth.

'Goodness me. Can that be young Robert Jackson? Well now, you must come along into the vicarage and get warm before the fire. You will get your death of cold out here.'

Robert followed the now-aged and shambling figure over the neatly mown grass and into the large ivy-covered rambling house where Mr and Mrs Forsyth lived and played their parts in the local community. Cups of tea and home-baked scones were soon produced and the years flew past in the conversation that followed.

'How is dear Caroline? And what of the children?' His sister Sophie and Master Nathaniel: 'Had they children?'

So many were the questions asked that Robert found it difficult to reverse the tables and ask about the village and its own inhabitants. But the 5.15pm train would not wait for him and it seemed far too soon that he was sat on it gazing out at the passing Cheshire countryside that he loved so well whilst on his way back to Liverpool. His ship back home was to sail with the morning tide next day. He had a trunk-full of presents to take back with him. A lace table-cloth for Caroline, a toy wooden fort for the boys and Macclesfield ribbons and some new bonnets for the girls.

It was to be Robert's only visit back to England. The company's demands on him took their toll as the years passed. After his loss of Caroline to cholera, one day in the late spring of 1896 Robert followed his beloved wife into the New England earth. For some years by then he had handed over the reins of the company to George and Matthew. Nat had retired earlier and none of his and Sophie's children seemed to be interested in the company. But George and Matthew, they were the future. Whilst Matthew had devoted all his time to the firm opening new branches both in the USA and even up in Canada, George had married Wilhelmina, a Canadian girl he had met whilst on business in Lower Canada and who was a daughter of Dutch immigrants into that country. They had been married in 1878 when George was at the age of 25 and it was their son – Leonard George – on whose shoulders lay the future of Jackson & Sons.

CHAPTER VIII

Canada 1912

In May 1904 Leonard George Jackson – third son of George James and his wife Wilhelmina – was married in the Protestant church of St Paul in Montreal, Canada. His father had prospered, and become one of the leading contractors to both the growing number of American railway companies and coastal steamship lines that served the towns and ports of New England and of the Maritime Provinces of Nova Scotia and New Brunswick in Canada. Leonard had been the family rebel ever since he was a small child. He was one who preferred to be on his own rather than join his brothers and sisters at playing games. At school he had been good at arithmetic and his watchful father had over the years come to respect his abilities and to mark him out as a future partner in the family business. Yet if Leonard was to be a partner he needed to have the benefits of discipline in business, and it was for that reason that, after Yale, he had been sent off to learn under an old friend of the family who ran a large grocery or "Italian Warehouse" in Canada.

There Leonard had met his future bride Clementine – "Clemmie" to her friends – and so another generation of the Jackson family had started to take shape. As a wedding present George and Wilhelmina had given the couple a modest amount of capital and bid them start their own branch of the family business in the still young new Dominion of Canada. Thereafter Leonard's aptitude for business soon showed itself capable of meeting the challenge and within a couple of years the new branch was able to report rising profits and the establishment of itself as a major supplier of a wide range of food and liquor as well as everything from ropes and canvas to deck-chairs and galley equipment for the ships that plied out of Montreal and Quebec City in summer; and out of the ice-free port of Halifax in Winter.

To keep the business going in winter the Montreal office also supplied many of the requirements of the railway companies that operated in Eastern Canada and over the border to the USA. One of the advantages of being based in Canada was that with Canada being part of British North America it was easier to import British goods and to get agencies to represent the firms and their brands. As time went on Leonard built up a network of contacts and agents all along the Atlantic seaboard of both countries especially for the items that he imported such as Scotch whisky and high quality china table-ware for ships. Especially when that was needed to replace items damaged in gales at sea when crossing the Atlantic.

When a ship arrived in Montreal it was as often as not that Leonard was the first person to be seen going up the gangplank to enquire of the ship's purser what new supplies would be needed. Often a bottle of Scotch or Bourbon for the purser, or even for the captain himself, could be seen peeping out of Leonard's frock coat as this young keen entrepreneur sought orders for victualling the ship. Indeed it was said that within a short space of time Leonard knew virtually every purser and every ship's captain on the Atlantic run. He knew their likes and their dislikes, and he knew their preferences in other ways as well. Many an early morning one or another young lady would call at his office to let him know that she was owed five dollars by the firm for services rendered the previous night on the SS something-or-other or at the Auberge des Cinq Étoiles.

Left to his own devices Leonard and the business prospered and branches sprung up or agencies were established in many places with Quebec City and Halifax being two of the most important. The time passed quickly and when Clementine produced their fourth child, Theodore, in early 1912 she and Leonard decided to celebrate by adding to their company headed notepaper and bills the description "Jackson and Company (Montreal) – ship's chandlers to the World". They were on their way.

Two days after Theodore was born at the family house in Sherbrooke Street in Montreal, Leonard left by train to visit his branches in Quebec and Halifax, Nova Scotia. The ice would soon be breaking up in the St Lawrence River. Then there would be the first ships passing Belle Isle and threading their way through the fogs off the Grand Banks whilst keeping a careful lookout for icebergs. He wanted to make sure that the Quebec office was ready for all the orders that might come its way. Once more the river would be filled with the sight of the masts of many a sailing ship and the plumes of smoke from the steamers that were heading up-river. The advent of spring also meant that there would be a little slackening off in the work at the Halifax office so it was a good time to check the inventories there and make decisions on whether to lay off some of the warehouse staff.

The visit to the Quebec office went well. He had a competent manager there, a Frenchman of about his own age. In Montreal much of the city's commercial life was dominated by the Scots who had settled there, and few of the top jobs went to the local French Canadians. But in Quebec the French were much more masters in their own chosen fields and Leonard, as an American by birth and upbringing, had little time for the national racial squabbles between the two groups that were the result of European history over the centuries.

On the 7th April 1912 Leonard checked out of his room at the Chateau Frontenac and took the train for Halifax. The plan was to spend the next week there. It was always pleasant to get away from the bitter cold of this city with its snow still piled high on the sidewalks and to get a spot of sea-air and feel that spring was on its way. Tomkins, who ran the Halifax operation, was a small bespectacled man in his early forties and who had a brother that worked for Leonard's father's firm in their New York office. At present the brother was on his way back there from London, England.

For three days Leonard worked meticulously through the sales and purchase ledgers each morning and in the afternoons he checked the stocks with Tomkins in the large brick warehouse down at the quayside. As ever things seemed in good order and his thoughts began to turn toward the return journey and the opportunity to once again see his new-born son. Clemmie would be glad to have him back. She always found the other two boys and their daughter Sophia quite a handful when he was away. At breakfast that morning in the hotel dining-room his mind was very much toying over the chance to perhaps get away a day early if he could get a berth on the overnight train to Montreal.

He finished his second cup of coffee and his toast and then looked at his gold pocket watch that his parents had given him for his twenty-first birthday. He frowned; by now

Tomkins should have arrived to pick him up so that they could talk privately together in the cab before reaching the office. Somewhat impatiently he once again glanced through the morning paper. He was always interested in the latest prices, be they those on the stock market or just the local cattle prices. He liked to have a feel for how all prices and the economy at large were moving so that he could perhaps be ahead of the game when negotiating in general. If markets were moving up then maybe his opponent across the table would be feeling more comfortable and relaxed and Leonard could squeeze an extra little out of the price he was being offered. If the general atmosphere of the markets was down then again the other man might be feeling depressed and Leonard could take advantage. After all business was business.

Having made sure he knew what the mood was locally from the paper he again glanced at the shipping news. There was a steamer due in from Liverpool, England and another from Le Havre in France; a couple of sailing barques were due to leave that day for the West Indies taking out lumber and maybe bringing back rum or sugar. The shipping news was a "must" for him to read when in any port. Where a steamship was coming from or a schooner or a clipper was leaving for, was part of Leonard's library of knowledge – his commercial bread and butter. Sometimes he would recognise the names of passengers disembarking from Europe in a place like Halifax. They would have time to spare awaiting the next train to Montreal, and if he had the opportunity and they were either personal friends or business clients, then Leonard would make time to call upon them in their hotel room.

The waiter, a small man with a large waxed moustache, as if all the hair on his head had migrated to below his nose, came over with the coffee pot. Leonard nodded, not really wanting the coffee but he had to occupy himself somehow.

'Dreadful thing, Sir,' murmured the waiter as the hot black-brown liquid was gently poured into the cup.

'What thing?' All of a sudden Leonard was very much alert.

'A ship, Sir.' The waiter straightened up.

'First we heard was when Chef arrived earlier to cook breakfast. His brother is a coastguard. They say a liner hit an iceberg in fog last night.'

He paused. 'Some say it was that new ship. What do they call her? "Titanic" or something? But that cannot be right. She is unsinkable. Isn't she Sir?'

The newly-poured coffee remained in the cup. The morning paper fell to the floor – and was trampled on – as Leonard headed for the lobby. Calling for his coat and gloves and placing his hat firmly on his head before tightly gripping the silver top of his walking cane, Leonard hurried through the revolving doors and down the steps to a waiting cab. After giving out instructions to the driver sitting up above he fell back into his seat as the cabbie, sensing the urgency, flipped his whip over the horse and they set off for the office at a cracking pace.

The next week was one that Leonard would never forget. During the first two days the enormity of the tragedy only started to sink in. That it was the Titanic that was the centre of the crisis was itself almost unbelievable. Halifax, like any other seaport, had had its share of maritime tragedies and suffering. Whether they had involved local fishermen lost in fogs on the Grand Banks or locally-based sailing ships that had foundered on some reef in the Caribbean or off West Africa the community had suffered. Such bad news and the loss of life was a part of everyday living in any sea-port. But a big liner sailing from England to New York was something else. That it was the Titanic – whose fame had crossed the Atlantic before she had even made her maiden voyage – was beyond credibility. Yet it was true, and the first bodies were already starting to be brought ashore.

By now the gentlemen of the press were starting to arrive in Halifax. The trains were coming in full of them. Some in their brown derby hats and with their note-books and pencils at the ever-ready had travelled up from Boston and New York. They were still dishevelled and half-asleep from the long journey but they were on the outlook for a human story. Any human story, true or not, would be sent back from the especially-installed telegraph office. The newspapers of Boston, of New York, Chicago and even San Francisco and the rest of the world were thirsty to know the latest. The Canadian press was also there in force and Leonard had had a long talk with a man from the Montreal Gazette whom he knew and whom he had chanced to meet in the street.

From the Gazette man Leonard had learned the names of some of the dead. It seemed as if almost every family of the great and the good of New York, of the rest of the USA and of Canada and England had suffered in some way. During those terrible days Leonard put himself at Tomkins' disposal. At first the poor man had been frantic, for he was not sure on which vessel his own brother was travelling back from England that week. Then a cable had arrived to say that he was not aboard the ill-fated liner and would be arriving in a few days' time.

Halifax itself did not know what had hit it. So many strangers in town. Every bed in every hotel and boarding house booked for the foreseeable future. Leonard was grateful that he had been able to keep his own room. At breakfast each morning the small bald-headed waiter with the waxed moustache was rushed off his feet and by the end of the first week Leonard could swear that the man had lost a good few pounds off his weight; although as if to compensate the poor man's income must have swollen with all the tips. The demands for re-fills of coffee at breakfast were phenomenal.

As he looked around the room Leonard could not help wondering, 'Was history being made that day? What would people think in a hundred years? Would they remember all of this?'

At the Ralston Building which housed the Halifax Hotel, and where many anxious family representatives were staying, an information bureau was set up to help the distraught relatives and visiting press. Extra telegraph lines had been installed at the Intercontinental Railway station for the world's newsmen and special trains were arriving all the time both bringing in the press and visitors and then taking away the corpses. On one track awaited a special train sent by the Grand Trunk Railway. This special had to sit and wait a few days before taking back the body of the Railway's own President, C.M. Hays. Eventually the train left for Montreal's Bonaventure station from where their chief was taken to the Mount Royal Cemetery high above that city.

Going about the city on his own company's business, Leonard would frequently pass the office at 1682 Hollis Street where the White Star Line, the owners of the Titanic, had their agents. Day and night the staff in the office worked frantically using the ship's manifest to help identify the bodies as they were brought ashore, then arranging funerals at the various churches in the town. The brunt of the services was born by the two Church of England buildings, St Paul's and St George's, together with the Roman Catholic St Mary's and the Nonconformist Brunswick Street Chapel.

One morning, five days after the sinking, Leonard was walking to the Halifax office. Obtaining a cab was virtually impossible, and in any case in the morbid atmosphere that was everywhere he found a little exercise and the fresh air was good for him. Leonard witnessed cart loads of coffins being taken to Karlsen's Wharf where the cable-ship Macay-Bennett had brought ashore 300 bodies and now was waiting to unload the corpses before returning to sea in the hope of finding further bodies. Another day, on his way back from luncheon, he witnessed a long line of hearses; the black plumes on the horses' heads seeming to perform a macabre dance as they set out from Coaling Wharf No. 4 where the bodies had been landed under military guard. The sad procession was on its way to the curling rink which had been commandeered as a temporary mortuary. To and from that place – where in much happier times Halifax families would go to celebrate birthday parties and other social and sporting gatherings – little family groups were now mournfully making their way in order to identify the bodies of their beloved ones; and to look upon them for the last time before handing them over to the funeral directors.

As one of the main ship's chandlers in the town, Tomkins and his staff were accustomed to acting in quick response to demands for their services from vessels low in supplies. Normally they held plenty of stocks but it was coming to the end of the season and many of the items had been run down. Now the sudden surge in requirements for everything from hurricane lamps to life belts and ropes of all thicknesses and qualities was unbelievable. Frequent trips to and from the site of the wreck by the various local and visiting ships meant the supply of all types of food and drink, especially beer for the hard-working crews, was equally in great demand. Leonard, his jacket off and his shirt sleeves pulled high by his expanding arm bracelets, worked into the night, often telling Tomkins that he could finish early and get back to his family about eight o'clock. He himself would frequently carry on with a skeleton staff until close to midnight. New supplies needed to be ordered by telegraph from the head office in Montreal so that they could be put on the next day's train. When Montreal could not help instructions were sent to branches in other ports including over the border in Portland, Boston and Providence. Some of the latter came by a specially chartered vessel that arrived late one night and was unloaded by the time dawn broke next morning.

Finally the supply situation started to come under control and the pressure eased. By May 9th, and three days after the special train of the Grand Trunk Railway had set off on its own sad journey to Montreal, Leonard at last felt able to return home. The back of the work had been broken, and that day as he walked out of the Railway Hotel holding his small brown portmanteau that had originally been designed to carry only enough clothes for a few days divided between Quebec City and Halifax, he crossed over Barrington Road and wearily descended the covered steps to North Street and its station. Glancing up at the clock on the tower above he knew that he had plenty of time before the Maritime Express left on its 846 mile journey that would take him back to home in Montreal.

Those five weeks from early April to almost the middle of May 1912 were ones that he would never forget. Later that evening he sat in the smoking car gazing out at the darkening passing countryside, where the first buds were opening on the trees. His mind could not get away from the thought that both out there hundreds of feet below the surface of the North Atlantic, and also in the graveyards of Halifax and by now countless other cemeteries throughout much of Eastern North America, lay young and old, poor and rich, the unknown (save to their own families) and the famous; none of whom would ever have the opportunity to see those early spring buds turn into the full beauty of vibrant summer. Nor would those good folk – for in death surely they were all good folk – ever again be able to look upon the wonderful colours of the fall.

Canada his adopted country, and the USA his true home, had had a horrible introduction to the second decade of the twentieth century. In time the wounds inflicted on society would heal, newly widowed men and women would find new spouses, and children without parents would themselves grow up and become true citizens in their communities.

Leonard said a silent prayer as he gazed out at those trees that spoke to the fortunate like him of spring. Peace would return, new ships would be built to carry more thousands at a time from old Europe to seek their fortunes in new North America. The USA would continue its march forward to greatness amongst the nations of the world. Canada, as part of the greatest Empire the world had ever known, would increase its wealth and prosperity as a trading nation. Yet as he looked through the glass of the train window he was aware of the reflection of himself; as if the future beyond the train was saying to him that never again must the world forget that the "unsinkable" could sink.

What, he mused as the train rumbled on into the darkness, did that future hold not just for himself and Clemmie but also for little Theodore, his two elder brothers and Sophia? Pray God there would be no more major tragedies to mar the hopes of this new twentieth century.

CHAPTER IX

A world-wide conflict, 1914-19

Four years later – almost to the day from when Leonard had seen those black-plumed horses drawing the hearses through the streets of Halifax carrying the pathetic remains from the Titanic's passengers – he once more was standing amongst the docks of Halifax gazing out into the harbour. It was most eerie for there on that May morning of 1916 it was almost as if the ghost of the Titanic had risen from the deep and at long last had made her way safely alongside the quay. But there were no cheering crowds to welcome her, no champagne receptions, no heavily bejewelled and be-furred women on the top deck gazing down as the ropes were wound round to hold her secure. No Captain Smith, bearded and slightly portly, on the Bridge and about to ring down 'Stop all Engines'. For this was not the Titanic but her sister ship "The Olympic". Canada was at war and the Olympic had been sent over to collect part of Canada's contribution for defending the Empire against the Kaiser's Germany.

There she was, tied up at the Deepwater Terminal, as Pier Number Two was called. Her four tall black funnels betraying just a wisp of smoke; her large anchor safely hauled in and tucked close to her almost vertical sharp bow, the two white decks of her superstructure above her black hull.

But there was a difference to the Titanic of that dreadful night four years ago. This time her lifeboats were hanging over the sides and the davits were swung out not in a desperate attempt to save as many passengers as possible but as a safety precaution against a possible torpedo attack from an enemy submarine. This time the decks were not crowded with frightened children whilst their mothers clung tightly to fathers who had already recognised that the cold sea was calling them to their deaths. Rather there was an atmosphere of bravado and elation as Canada – youthful Canada – was setting off to war.

Now the decks were crowded with the monotonous colour of khaki-brown from the uniforms of the multitude of young men's faces that were to be seen above the rails. It was clear for all to see that the passengers on this voyage would no longer be the rich and the famous, the commercial traveller and the would-be immigrant. This time they would be thousands of troops, drawn from all over Canada, and off to help save the Empire on the already blood-soaked fields of France.

Just under two years earlier Leonard and his family had been down in the States visiting his parents on holiday in Maine when the morning newspaper had reported, in a small item on an inside page, that some Archduke – Leonard did not know what an "archduke" was or did, but it sounded rather grand and typically European – had been assassinated at a place called Sarajevo. A couple of weeks later when they got back for luncheon from the beach and looked at the paper that never arrived at their holiday home until mid-morning they read that Great Britain and France were at war with the Kaiser's Germany. They went off for their picnic that afternoon blissfully unaware that those reports from Europe, and which by now had managed to get on the front page of the newspapers, were to alter all their lives and the lives of generations to come.

The beginning of September 1914 saw Leonard and Clemmie back in Montreal and business once more getting into gear. But there was an odd atmosphere in Canada that contrasted with that south of the border. Canada was, of course, part of the British Empire and there was a feeling abroad in society that they had a duty to support England in her fight with the Hun. There were in Canada these days a fair number of Germans living in the country, but then there was even more French – especially in cities such as Montreal and Quebec – so there was no doubt on which side of the contest Canada would find itself. Canadians were in fact British subjects and owed their loyalty to the King of England, King George V. But back in the States the population was a much larger mixture drawn from so many countries and moreover there was no specific loyalty to any overseas king. After all it was only 100 years ago that the two countries had been at war and even the very border between Canada and the USA had been in dispute. Essentially, as Leonard's father George had said, this was a war between European nations. 'And even so,' his wife Wilhelmina had pointed out from her knowledge of her own Dutch ancestry, 'it was only some of the big nations that were involved. Holland, for example, would be neutral like the United States.'

However on their return to Montreal Leonard and Clemmie had discovered a very different attitude. For Canadians it was a case that the mother country – England – was under threat. The "Hun", with his infamous spiked helmet, had invaded poor little Belgium – Holland's neighbour – and was already on French soil heading for Paris.

As the last few months of 1914 rolled over into the following year military uniforms were starting to be seen on the city streets and even train-loads of soldiers were quite common in the stations of Canadian towns. Leonard was not one to miss out on the commercial opportunities that might arise from such a significant development as a war. By the early summer of 1915 he had already landed a considerable number of contracts to supply the troop ships that were taking members of the CEF – the Canadian Expeditionary Force – across the Atlantic.

He had wondered whether to go to the extreme and actually enlist and get a post as a "supplies officer" but there were two snags to that thought. Firstly he was a citizen of the US and thus the very thought of attesting loyalty to another country and its Emperor King was somewhat galling to him, and secondly if he was to be in uniform he would have his freedom to organise supplies severely curtailed. Instead he would retain his freedom of action but become a commissary support civilian. For technical reasons he would wear an officer's uniform but only in extreme circumstances would he be subject to military law. In all but name he would still be a civilian and free to operate commercially to the best of his ability in supplying food and drink to the troop ships, their crews and the men that they carried.

So as to meet his new role he had had to spend a long weekend at a military camp in the Eastern Townships in order to be fitted with his uniform and to learn basic army procedures; then he had returned to his own desk and carried out his normal business. Tomkins, still in charge at the Halifax office, was extremely busy supplying the many warships and merchant navy vessels that were using that port. There had been some complaints that the troops were not getting sufficient rations for their crossings to Great Britain and so Leonard had decided to make a trip over with them and see what they needed and whether the supplies to the vessels were sufficient. Thus it was that one April day in 1916 Leonard – now thirty two years of age and thus slightly older than most of his travelling officer companions – boarded a train for Halifax. He would spend a couple of months there studying the supply situation before making the crossing to England.

It was exactly midday that train No. 34 of the Intercolonial Railway Company pulled out of Montreal station to make its first stop at St Hyacinthe on the opposite bank of the St Lawrence river. Just before midnight, and twelve hours into the long journey, the train stopped at Rimouski having earlier called numerous times in the first 343 miles.

Leonard was tired by now. He had tried to get to sleep earlier but attached to the train were some cars full of troops, themselves also on their way to Halifax. Their singing and laughter seemed to go on for hours until the Goddess of Sleep finally and mercifully closed Leonard's eyes. Dawn saw them at Dalhousie Junction after a further 100 miles and the conductor reminded his passengers that it was now Atlantic Time and they must adjust their pocket-watches. Onwards they trundled through the vast forested landscapes. Patches of snow still lay on the ground on north-facing slopes but as they progressed further and further east there began to be signs of spring in the countryside through which the "Maritime Express" was making its stately passage. Leonard visited the Dining Car for breakfast and by mid-morning they were in Moncton and with 650 miles behind them since they had left Montreal the previous day. At 15.30 they halted at Truro. Further down the train the noisy soldiers who had kept Leonard awake the previous evening were all clambering out and an enterprising one amongst them had produced a camera for a group photograph. What, Leonard wondered, would be the destiny of all those fine young men who with confidence and high hopes were off to fight for The Empire in a foreign land? Taking the opportunity to likewise stretch his legs by walking up and down the platform he struck up a casual conversation with two of the young men. He learned that the group were not regular soldiers of the Canadian Army but instead were volunteers from McGill University back in Montreal. They had been formed into an artillery battery and were on their way to the next stage of their training at The Citadel in Halifax. Leonard could not help but admire these young men who had chosen to put their careers on hold, maybe even to sacrifice their lives, for what they felt was a just cause.

Two hours later there was a smell of sea air wafting into the car through the open window and the train was being accompanied by a number of wheeling and swooping seagulls as she slowed down and cautiously picked her way amongst the myriad of tracks into Halifax's North Street station. The large station building, constructed in the Victorian Gothic style, always reminded Leonard of the first Grand Central Station in New York. Outside in the forecourt were a number of civilian automobiles together with a handful of army vehicles. As an American, Leonard was always fascinated that Canada had chosen to use right-hand drive vehicles like the mother country the other side of the Atlantic, rather than left-hand drive ones as in the USA.

The 'Select Fifty' at Truro on the way to Halifax, Nova Scotia, May 1916.

German prisoners-of-war. The Citadel, Halifax, Nova Scotia, 1916.

Barrack-room at The Citadel, Halifax, Nova Scotia, May 1916.

A practice dug-out being examined by visiting relatives from Montreal before embarkation for France in the Fall of 1916.

Army catering 1916-style. A lot of potatoes to peel!

Ewshot Camp, Surrey, England, November 1916.
Gunners: E.F. Christian, J.D.M.B. Beattie, E.S.Marriotte, R. Reid, J.A. Ferguson, R. Symonds, A.H. Chisolm

Ready to move off: the 'Select Fifty' with full gear preparing to march, 1916.

To war with modern army transport, 1916-17.

'Olympic', sister ship of the ill-fated 'Titanic' in Halifax, September 1916.

And so to war. McGill Overseas Battery, Siege Artillery, Canadian Expeditionary Force (CEF) with horse-drawn transport, 1917.

To the front line. France, 1917.

The results of war. France, February 1918.

All photos in this section are reproduced by kind permission of the author's family.

It was with a sigh of relief that Leonard was finally able to stretch himself fully as he descended from the maroon car onto the platform and he gave a friendly wave of thanks to the engine-man on the footplate of the big black locomotive that had hauled them nearly 850 miles in just over a day and a half. At least he had been able to travel in comfort making use of the sleeping car and the on-board dining service but he wondered how those brave khaki-clad fellows further back had fared. Tomkins was on the platform to greet him and they took a waiting cab straight to his normal hotel.

For the next few weeks and into the summer months Leonard shared the duties of organising and supplying visiting vessels with all manner of foodstuffs and liquor and beer. The volumes seemed vast compared to the old days of peace-time and the firm had to widen the net of their suppliers to find new companies who could give them the extra amounts that wartime needs required. There was also the fact that ships from different nations often wanted items that were not to be found on the routine lists of the major wartime vessels. Fish was always in demand, but how did you satisfy the Scottish master who wanted haggis for his crew who would be in the Indian Ocean on a forthcoming Burns' Night?

Eventually in early September Leonard received a note to say that the "Olympic" was about to sail. She was to carry a large contingent of the Canadian Expeditionary Force to England. As one of the largest ships afloat in the world, she would be carrying thousands of troops and so would give Leonard a good opportunity to study the varying needs of supplies for such large numbers. Given his nominal rank as a major (commissariat) Leonard was given an outside cabin on the port side. He shared it with a professor of medicine from Toronto who was being sent over to inspect the health conditions on board and the camp hygiene for Canadian troops in both England and France. Like himself, the professor had to wear military uniform to meet the regulations. These two "civilian soldiers", as they dubbed themselves, enjoyed each other's company as they walked about the first class deck discussing the war. They dined in the large restaurant with generals and brigadiers who were well aware of the need to "keep sweet" these two men whose missions were to ensure the troops had good health and plenty to eat.

On disembarking at Liverpool Leonard was met by the local Canadian government representative and another man who turned out to be one of the leading ship's chandlers in that great British seaport. The next week was spent coming to a commercial agreement on mutual help for each other's firms. Wilkins and his Liverpool office would take responsibility for restocking the west-bound troop ships in Liverpool before they set off back to collect more of the CEF. He would also ensure that his staff and colleagues in their London and Southampton offices would do the same. In return Leonard's offices in Halifax, Montreal and Quebec would be responsible for supplying goods that were ordered by telegraph from England for vessels where Wilkins had the contracts. By the end of September Leonard was once more on board ship. On a smaller vessel of the Allen Line, the "Corsican", he was once more heading out of Liverpool, this time back directly to Montreal. In November he was again in Halifax and went on board the "Empress of Britain" which was also being used as a troop transport vessel.

But it was before sailing to Liverpool on his study-trip, and whilst having a drink one evening with Tomkins in the bar of the hotel in which he was staying, that he recognised a group of faces from that photo-stop of the train at Truro earlier in the spring. Although most men of their military rank would not normally have gained access to a bar that was usually the territory of only officers, these "gunners" all could boast university degrees and an academic knowledge of the world that was the superior of many a lieutenant or captain whom they had to salute on the barrack square or in the street. One twenty-year old, who obviously hailed from a good family in Montreal, told Leonard that the coming voyage was not his first across the Atlantic. He had been a couple of times in the past to visit his parents' family over in Scotland. Leonard had little doubt that the young man in question had been used to travelling first class and this was confirmed when by chance the man mentioned his father by name and Leonard knew him to be one of the leading members of the Scottish commercial community in Montreal.

After arriving in Halifax, the group told Tomkins and Leonard that they had been stationed at The Citadel and there taught how to fire their guns. They had put down their text books to join the Expeditionary Force and were now conversant with the language of "12-pounders" and of "4.7 guns". They knew the difference between a breech and a muzzle and could fire a "B.L. Howitzer" almost without blinking an eyelid. Only twelve months before, they had all been hard at studying everything from ancient Greek to the latest theories of chemistry. During their time at The Citadel the men had been able to get some vacation leave whilst awaiting embarkation and the young man whom Leonard had befriended told him how his family has come down by train from Montreal and had spent a few weeks on holiday in the area. He had had permission to spend his furlough with them at Chester where they had all been sailing to places such as Oak Island, or going for walks amongst the woods on the Peninsula.

Now by August they were all back in the South Barrack and had been warned that they would sail for England the next month. In his room that evening, before turning out the lamp Leonard thought of all those young men from McGill University. The very academic flowering of modern Canada and now destined – at their own choice – for the bloodied battlefields of France. How long would this terrible war last? And would those beautiful petals of Canadian intelligentsia wither and die amongst the mud of a Flanders field? Or would they perhaps survive and be the leaders of a Canada of this new twentieth century? And what if the German Kaiser would win and the British Empire go down in the same way as had the Titanic? Would a successful Kaiser's Germany come to rule Canada? Should that be a threat, would the USA allow it or would perhaps after all his own beloved USA have to step in and sort out these squabbling European nations? He turned out the lamp in his room and as he did so he was reminded of the story he had read in a newspaper when last in England of how, as War was the declared in 1914, the British Foreign Secretary had said, 'Tonight the lamps are going out all over Europe.' It was a troubled Leonard that went to sleep that night in his hotel in Halifax.

As ever with any war there were losers and gainers both in the military field and amongst those whose commercial interests were affected. For Leonard and his Canadian company the last two years through to 1918 were ones of considerable financial progress in supplying the navy and the army but their achievements were nothing by comparison to those of his father's organisation over the border. The entry of the US into the war in 1917 saw a tremendous increase in demand for the services of the company and its commercial competitors. Then, eventually, came that November day in 1918 when at long, very long, last the next round of ammunition was not needed to be put in the breech of the howitzers and the next whistle indicating once again the soldiers were to scramble up the ladders over the muddy sides of the trenches and go forward into a hail of enemy fire was no longer blown. The silence was beyond belief to those for whom such sounds and activities had become a way of life – and of death.

Leonard was later to learn that those young McGill artillery men had fought at Vimy, that French ridge that overlooked the frontier between the French Republic and the German-occupied monarchy of Belgium. It was a long time since they had all happily tumbled out of the troop train at Truro for a "family" photograph. After landing in England during the fall – or autumn as the British called it – of 1916 they had been sent to Witley camp in Surrey in the south of the country and not far from the coast. On a quiet day when the wind was gently blowing over the English Channel from a France only 30 odd miles away they could sometimes hear the "crump, crump" of explosions. Later they moved to another camp nearby at Ewshot where once more they were subjected to training with their guns. They managed to get some leave and those fortunate to have friends or relatives would slip away to visit them, yet always still in uniform and needing to salute every officer that they passed in the street. The turn of the year had seen the unit transferred to yet another camp at Lydd on the English Kent coast and then a move over the Channel to France and eventually to that hell-hole of Vimy Ridge. That same young man from whom Leonard learned of the events of those years had been wounded and after treatment in a field hospital was sent to the main allied hospital on the coast at Etaples. From there he was evacuated back to Norwich in Eastern England and where the local lunatic asylum had been converted for military use. Once more fit to fight he had returned to Vimy where the frontlines of Canadian and German troops had scarcely moved during the months of his convalescence. Indeed so close were the Canadian and German trenches that during the occasional lulls in fighting at night the troops in each side could hear the others talking. Then came that wonderful November 11th of 1918 when the guns fell permanently silent. Once more the Battery of those young McGill men returned to England to then be shipped back home in January of the following year.

Just as Canadian soldiers were to do again less than a quarter of a century later, in 1919 the young soldiers of the Canadian Expeditionary Force marched proudly through Montreal. Their shoulders were straight, their heads held high and their uniforms showed not a stain of French mud nor a forgotten crease as they stepped smartly along behind the bands in the Victory Parade.

CHAPTER X

Peace, but not Prosperity

The immediate years after the peace were ones of continued prosperity for Leonard's firm. New branches were opened, including over in Vancouver on Canada's Pacific coast, and as the family wealth grew so did the plans for the next generation to join the company. Theodore, now a strapping twenty-five-year-old, had been studying at Yale when suddenly one evening in 1929 he received a telephone call from his father in New York. Share prices had suddenly dropped on Wall Street, the firm had received seven order cancellations that day and his father was worried. Within days the crisis was the main topic in all the newspapers both sides of the border and ships were cutting their requirements as the cancellation of passenger reservations flowed in. Plans were hastily changed, the firm could not afford extra new staff and so Theo decided to go into teaching instead. People would always need to be educated and whilst the rewards might not be as financially satisfying there was the compensation of job security in those uncertain days.

So Theo obtained a post at one of the many preparatory schools for boys that catered for the sons of wealthy New England families. He had majored in modern languages – French, German and Italian – and he spent his days teaching these to the fourth and fifth grades until the youngsters left the preparatory school and headed towards their last few years before later proceeding to one of the ivy-league colleges such as Princeton, Harvard or his own alma mater of Yale in nearby New Haven, Connecticut.

Whilst Theo was beavering away moulding his students for their future careers, the New Deal of President Franklin D Roosevelt was likewise moulding the America around all of them. As time went on, and on the days when Theo had to visit New York City, he started to notice that the bread-lines and soup-kitchens seemed to be getting less, both in their lengths and in their numbers. Of course the problems of unemployment were still all around. Many folk seemed to avoid the street-cars to save the odd dime and would walk to work instead. But in the evenings many of the shows on Broadway were once again open, and the lights were on. Outside fashionable night-clubs and hotels the wealthy women – or at least those women who were trying to give the impression of again being wealthy – were to be found stepping out of cabs dressed in their long satin gowns and with furs draped over their comely shapes. There was always a top-hatted beau at their side and from time to time Theo, from the opposite sidewalk, would recognise a father of one of his pupils, but not always with the lady who came to the school at the end of term.

Scenes of that nature would sometimes make Theo stop and ponder as to the future of his own students of a particular year. Was all the sweat and grind of his teaching, and indeed of the boys' learning French, German and Italian, a waste of money and time? Would many of those in his care ever see those countries in far-off Europe? In another fifteen years would those same boys be the ones stepping out of a cab with a product of Chapin, Spence or any of the other big private girls' schools at their side and without having once had the need to speak any of the languages that Theo had drilled into them?

It was thoughts of such nature, together with the hope that a practical experience of the countries might encourage the work ethic in a ten- or eleven-year-old, that made Theo determined to start a series of visits to Europe during the summer vacations in the early 1930s. He would take perhaps thirty or forty boys with him. They would cross the Atlantic on one of the smaller less-expensive liners and work their way through the different countries. In the years after they were married his new wife Henrietta would accompany him and add a little of a "motherly" touch to the benefit of those missing home on their first visit abroad.

They would tour the main cities of far-off Europe seeing the sights and sometimes visiting the occasional foreign school. Once landed, they would stay at small hotels that catered for school parties and of course they would always travel between towns and cities by train.

Their marriage was in early 1936, just before FDR gained his second term in the White House by beating the republican Alfred Landon. That year, on the school's visit to Germany, Theo could not help noticing something of a difference about the atmosphere in the cities. The number of boys on the trip had been reduced at the last moment when the sons from a number of wealthy Jewish families suddenly pulled out. The reasons given by the parents were varied but Theo could not help feeling that the news from Germany was not helping. The plan was to sail to Le Havre in France and then on by train to Paris, before Berlin and Leipzig in Germany and finally to Rome, Italy before returning to Paris and back to New York.

As ever Paris welcomed its arms to the young American visitors. They visited the Eiffel Tower and the Tomb of the Emperor Napoleon at Les Invalides before making the long walk up the Avenue Champs Elysée to the grand arch at its head with all the names of Napoleon's battles inscribed on the white granite surfaces. This was all great stuff. French schools did not go on vacation until just before August so their visit starting in early July enabled Theo to have also arranged a couple of short visits to schools in the city. One was in the wealthy 8th Arrondissement, as the Parisians called their districts, whilst the other was on the south eastern outskirts of the city where the children came from poor and middle class families who had been badly affected by the unemployment of recent years.

But the visit to Germany thereafter was somewhat unsettling to at least Theo and Henrietta, if not to the boys. The party were turned out of their overnight "couchette" sleeper car at the German border whilst the valises were soundly examined by border guards and their passports checked by menacing looking officials who wore swastika armbands to show their authority. In the early morning as the train approached Berlin one of the new autobahn highways could be seen. Once they had arrived, the streets of the capital city seemed full of uniformed figures, soldiers, Nazi troopers and policemen. A planned visit to a school was suddenly cancelled with no explanation. Everywhere that they went they seemed to be being watched by men in long raincoats and with hats that obscured their faces. It was with relief that after three days Theo saw them all safely on the train and heard the wail of the engine whistle as the long steam train pulled out of the station and headed for Leipzig.

The beautiful South-German city with its fine buildings seemed a relief by comparison to the overbearing atmosphere in the capital. The boys wandered around the Augustplatz with its fine fountain and floral beds of summer flowers. The masses of coloured plants were sparkling as ever despite the summer heat, whilst the blue street-cars were wending their way through the tree-lined avenues. One evening Henrietta and Theo managed to slip away on their own from the hotel in the Leibniz-Strasse and wander round the Johanna Park with its lovely lake and whose banks were adorned by magnificent trees sweeping down to the water's edge. On the Sunday they all attended morning service at the English church in the city.

Three days later they were crossing the Alps – Europe's closest thing to the Rockies – which divides the colder and wetter northern Europe from the warm Mediterranean sea-washed shores that lie off the northern coast of Africa.

Rome saw some of the boys suffering upset stomachs and the ministrations of Henrietta were much in demand; but they soon recovered and all went together to the Sistine Chapel in The Vatican, where they were fortunate enough to catch a glimpse of the pontiff Pope Pius the Eleventh. One day the party witnessed a military parade in celebration of some Italian hero from the recent 1915-1918 war. The small uniformed figure of the Italian King Victor Emanuel took the salute, but he seemed dwarfed both in height and presence by someone behind him.

'Who is that?' asked Henrietta quietly in Theo's ear, 'The funny-looking tall fat figure in a hat with a tassel down its side?'

'Shssh!' responded her husband, 'That is the dictator, Benito Mussolini.'

On other years the annual vacation took them first to London or to the Dutch city of Amsterdam and then to one or another of the main capital cities or cultural centres of Europe such as Florence in Italy and Salzburg in Austria. Yet as the years passed by there seemed to be a growing uneasiness over there and it seemed each time more and more comforting to be back home when the ship passed the Statue of Liberty and they entered the Hudson.

The visit of 1938 had been particularly disturbing. Hitler had marched into Czechoslovakia in the spring of that year and they had found that their travel agents had re-routed their rail journey at the last minute so as to avoid that part of Central Europe. They made an unscheduled stop at the northern Italian city of Verona where Henrietta had suggested a visit to the Forum, a vast tall arena that had originally been built by the Romans in about 200 AD. It had served as the main theatre for both the local citizens and the occupying Roman soldiers, for it was where spectacles were held that ranged from gladiatorial fights to scenes of Christians being thrown to the lions as a punishment for them taking up the new religion of that faith. Sitting high up on the stone seats the boys had allowed their imaginations to run riot. But at least it was giving the youngsters the idea of life in a different age and it perhaps also made them feel the many benefits of living in a secure and safe country like their own blessed USA.

By the summer of 1939 most of the world had begun to realise that war in Europe was an inevitability. Nonetheless almost every American was sure that it would be another squabble amongst the old nations of the world. Many were firmly convinced that this time round the New World – or at least the USA – would be able to keep clear of any entanglements. On the fastest of passenger liners Europe was still five days sailing away from the East Coast. Their different histories, cultures and languages made the arguments between those far-off nations, many of whom were smaller than many an American state, virtually unintelligible to the man back home. Of course it was interesting to visit these countries on vacation, but as to their politics, 'no, thank you!' America still had enough to do pulling itself up by its bootstraps from the ravages of the Great Depression. Besides there was that new movie just come to town and there was the State Fair due in a few weeks. Let those Europeans sort themselves out!

That last summer, before those nations of Frenchman, German, Hollander and Brit started to tear each other to shreds, saw Theo and Henrietta take another party over in the month of July. They sailed on a Cunarder to Liverpool, England and as the vessel tied up at the Pier Head the boys were intrigued to see a tall black office-block building atop of which were a couple of large green birds. They were told they were "Liver birds", the emblem of that great British port.

This was the very same port from which Theo's ancestors had sailed to the USA nearly a century before. The thought of that sent a tingle down his back. Behind the building ran an elevated railroad, rather similar to that back in New York, but which covered some 14 miles of docks facing the River Mersey

136

into which they had sailed earlier that day. Henrietta had never been to England before and she was fascinated to observe the English and their manners and habits. No "gentleman" would enter an elevator in which there were ladies (always "ladies" not "women") without first removing his hat. Black "bowler" hats were the normal wear amongst such men-folk and the accents of the women rather reminded Henrietta of the seagulls that had accompanied the liner once it neared land. 'Eow…this' and 'Eow…that' sounded so like the screeches of the birds that had swooped for food thrown by passengers from the elevated decks of the liner.

English "Society" seemed as much divided by classes as back home. But there was a difference. The English seemed to have some mystical method of classifying people by such things as their accents and little mannerisms. Amongst the latter was the question of on which finger a man wore a wedding-ring. Wealth – the normal means of distinguishing oneself from the next person in the America of the 1930s – and the clothes worn were almost secondary in England. The school a person had been at, the house they lived in and whether they hunted foxes were the accepted tell-tale marks that divided up the different English classes. Clothes most certainly did not matter. A Duke (whatever that was), when he was not wearing his coronet, or a "lord" when he was not in the House of Lords – their equivalent of the Senate back in Washington DC – could wear any old clothes. The only way you could tell him from his gardener was when he opened his mouth, although most English accents were a little difficult to understand to a modern American. The English "class" thing was a very funny system to comprehend.

Theo and Henrietta and the boys travelled the two hundred miles down to London by train the day after they had arrived at Liverpool. Naturally as Americans they and the youngsters travelled "First Class". It seemed you either travelled "First Class" or "Third Class". Theo had remarked that perhaps this was a subtle way of keeping the different segments of society over there very much apart. It was most odd. How much better to have "Pullman" or "Coach"? But "Class"…! And what had happened to the "Second Class" travellers – did none exist? Who did they used to be? Thank goodness they lived in a democracy back in New England.

In London everyone was a little on edge and seemed to be expecting war to start any time. There were practice air raid warnings with sirens sounding over the town, and in the parks they saw air raid shelters being dug. Three days in that atmosphere was enough. The boys had seen Buckingham Palace where the newly crowned King George lived. Many of them had already seen the king when he and his Queen Elizabeth had been Stateside recently to visit the President. Then Theo had taken the youngsters to the Houses of Parliament, England's Congress. They had sat in the "Strangers Gallery" and seen the British Prime Minister, Mr Neville Chamberlain, talking about the situation in Europe. It was interesting to see a place that they had heard of when back home but it all looked rather dull and dreary. Dreary that was until they went into the "House of Lords". You could hear the boys take a deep breath as they saw all the red benches where the lords and dukes and others sat. There were even some bishops there in their long white robes. But the thing that really took away their breath were the two golden thrones at the far end of the room. There were two of them because, it was explained to them, one was each for the king and the queen. It was almost fairyland coming alive. England was a very different country to their own back home.

One morning a few days later they were at London's Victoria Station by nine o'clock in order to get their reserved seats on the "boat train" to France. After a two hour journey they arrived at Dover where they got out of the train and walked straight to the ferry-boat alongside the platform. The crossing of the English Channel itself was also to take about two hours from Dover to the French port of Calais. As the steamer left the Western Pier and sailed out of the harbour into a fairly choppy English Channel, Theo looked up at the high white cliffs of Dover that seemed to dominate the busy little town and its bustling seaport. As he gazed up at the chalk cliffs that had once upon a time joined England and France together, Theo had a funny feeling. A sort of anticipatory shudder crossed his shoulders and seemed to set his spine a-tingle as he looked up at those tall white cliffs with their one thousand year old castle perched up at the top. It was an odd feeling and one Theo could not understand. It was a feeling that he would not forget but which he would not understand. Not until when one night a few years later, this time in the cockpit of a bomber and once more heading for France, he looked down through a gap in the clouds and in the pale moonlight saw the same white cliffs fast fading into the background as he left England yet again – but this time on a deadly mission.

Three of the boys were seasick on that ferry as they crossed from Dover that day. But the sight of the French port cheered them up and in no time they were clambering up into their seats on the passenger train at the Gare Maritime. The big French engine – those French trains and their locos were much larger than the ones on which they had travelled in England – was snorting with steam as it started its slow journey over the port tracks before then gathering up speed heading for first the city of Amiens then on to the French capital, Paris, about three hours away.

Paris in that summer of 1939 was as much on edge as had been London. But there was a marked difference in the atmosphere between the two. There seemed to be much more social tension in France. One day they had to walk everywhere all day as the Paris Metro – the city's subway – was on strike; and it seemed there were other strikes all over the place. In England there had seemed – at least to Theo – to be a resignation that war was to come. That other side of the Channel the feeling had been accompanied by a grim determination to all pull together and prepare for it. It had taken the Brits a long time to accept that the danger was there; but once they had come to terms with what seemed inevitable they were getting stuck in. In Paris it was all still a matter of doubt and argument and everywhere there were differing opinions on how to react. The French army seemed prepared for war. It was a common sight to see trucks of fully kitted-out soldiers dodging in and out of the city's traffic and narrowly avoiding the green-bodied, cream-roofed buses with open-ended rear platforms full of gesticulating travellers. At every major road junction stood a French "gendarme" or policeman directing the traffic. No gendarme was complete without his funny looking flat circular hat and his white gloves that tightly gripped an equally white baton. That baton was used to tell the automobiles and other vehicles when to stop or to proceed to the accompaniment of short blasts on a whistle apparently permanently gripped between each gendarme's teeth.

It had been agreed at the school before the party had sailed for Europe that England and France were to be the only countries to be visited due to the worrying international situation. Of course as Americans they were neutral and not involved but even so it had been an almost unanimous decision by parents and school authorities alike that they would not venture that year as far as the Fascist countries of Germany – which the previous year had swallowed-up Austria – and Italy. Just as whilst in Great Britain they had toured cities such as York, Chester and Edinburgh so when in France they had ventured beyond Paris to the old silk-making town of Lyon and then down to the smart Mediterranean seaside holiday resorts of the French Riviera. The days soon passed and little by little the French accents of the boys improved and their knowledge of the language widened. Or so it seemed until in Paris one late August night just before they were due to set off back to the US two of the boys got separated from the rest. They had all split up into groups and were due to meet at one of the Metro stations at 5pm to go back to their hotel near the Arc de Triomphe. Two members of one of the groups had decided they wanted a second look at some "rather interesting" posters outside a theatre in the Montmartre area where they had spent the afternoon. Finding themselves lost amongst an area full of rather seedy theatres and with time running out they did what they felt was the only sensible thing. They asked their way by going up to passers-by and saying, 'La guerre? La guerre?' Of course they had meant 'la gare' – 'the station'. In their schoolboy French they had managed to say 'the war' and by themselves those two Connecticut teenagers almost brought the world war to a premature start. For a few minutes Gallic panic reigned throughout Montmartre. There and then when he later heard of the episode Theo resolved that next year – if there was to be a next year – a little extra coaching would be necessary.

That Saturday afternoon on 2nd September 1939 when Theo and Henrietta saw the ropes holding the liner to the French quayside at Cherbourg dropping away they both had feelings in the pits of their stomachs that there would be no school visit next year. At the Paris station of Gare St Lazare the French newspapers that morning had been full of reports that Germany had invaded Poland. France and Great Britain were supposed to be pledged to stand beside Poland in the event of such an attack, rather as they had both done when they had supported Belgium in 1914.

That time the Germans had conquered Belgium and invaded France. Of course they had been halted after advancing a fairly short distance and both sides had spent most of the next four years fighting to a standstill in the muddy trenches of northern France. The boys knew from their history lessons that the fighting had been stalemate until General Pershing and the American Army had come to the rescue of the French and British and had driven the Germans back out of France and into defeat. Surely it would not mean all that again? Surely none of those boys down on "E" Deck would be involved in a few years' time?

On the way over at the start of the holiday Theo had been playing bridge on the ship and the talk had turned to discussing the part America had played in the previous War. The two English men at the table had been of the opinion – although they had put it as politely as they found able – that the US had only joined in at the last moment so that they could get some advantage from the peace negotiations that were to follow the final outcome. Funny ideas that some Brits had about history!

All of this floated briefly through Theo's mind as he saw the ropes at Cherbourg fall away severing the final physical links with the mainland of Europe. There was another liner tied up at the next mooring on the quayside, its decks crammed with French men and women. It was said that it was going to a French colony in the Caribbean and that many on board were Jewish families putting the Atlantic Ocean between them and the menace of Nazi Germany. It was a lovely evening as the big American passenger liner passed the final promontory of French land. Coming in the opposite direction they met a large cruiser which was entering the harbour. The naval personnel – or "matelots" as the French called them – all dressed in smart uniforms that included flat white caps complete with a red bobble on the top, could be seen scurrying around the decks preparing for their vessel to tie up. The Captain of the American liner dipped his ship's flag in salute and Theo could clearly see the navy Captain on the other ship give a magnificent smart salute in return before following it with a friendly wave. What, Theo wondered, would lie in the future for that brave captain, his crew and their battle-grey warship if France went to war?

Every day as the liner progressed over the ocean heading for New York the news in the ship's newspaper got more grim. In the Monday morning edition it was said that England had

143

finally declared war on Germany in support of beleaguered Poland. Perhaps those practice air raid warnings and the bomb-shelters that they had seen in those London parks were going to be needed after all. A general quiet hush seemed to have cast itself upon all on board.

Theo and Henrietta had discussed the situation on the first night at sea and they had agreed not to say anything to the boys about the dangers of being at sea in wartime. Neither of them could forget what had happened to the liner Lusitania in the last war when she had been torpedoed and hundreds of innocent American and other passengers had lost their lives. Of course everybody on board their own ship had been a little bit jittery when boat-drill had been carried out on the first day at sea. However, whether out of fear or perhaps superstition, it seemed the word "submarine" was not to be found on the lips of anyone, even if it lay dormant in most minds. Nothing was said but Theo drew comfort when he noted that the ship's captain had all lights blazing at night as she sailed through a glassy sea. He was especially relieved to see there was a searchlight specially trained on the large Old Glory flying from the stern. She was an American ship and America was a neutral in this squabble amongst all those Europeans they had now left far astern. Long may she stay a neutral.

Friday morning saw them entering The Narrows and a short while later Lady Liberty could be clearly seen on the port side as they made their way through the early-morning mists and entered the Hudson river. They were HOME and they were ALL SAFE. God Bless America.

CHAPTER XI

Italy 1944

In 1995 James had taken Helen on holiday to Europe to celebrate their wedding anniversary. Helen's grandparents had been born in Italy and had first set foot on American soil on Ellis Island during the 1930s. Helen had always wanted to see the country that the family still referred to as "home" – "nostra patria". James had his own reasons for also wanting to see Italy but that was a piece of family history that he had diplomatically kept to himself when he first met his future parents-in-law and later on he had somehow never gotten round to mentioning it to them.

Way back in 1944 James' father Theodore had also visited Italy, but not by choice. He had been part of an aircrew that had been shot down whilst taking part in a bombing raid over Italy.

In the summer of the previous year, 1943, American forces had invaded Sicily, the big island at the "toe" of Italy. The invasions had been the first real step to liberating Europe and the first when large numbers of Allied troops had actually set foot on the enemy-occupied European mainland. They had earlier landed in North Africa and had met up with the British who had fought their way all along the northern coast of that continent from Egypt. Sicily had fallen after fierce fighting and then at Anzio the Allies had landed only a short distance south of Rome. The Italians had quickly capitulated and then joined the Allies against Germany. But there were German divisions strung out across the middle of Italy preventing the invading American and British armies advancing up the "leg" of that country. The Italian dictator, Benito Mussolini, had fled north with the help of his German protectors and had set up a Fascist government in a small pre-war holiday town on the side of Lake Garda in the north of Italy and very near the old Austrian border. It was a town called Salo.

Day by day, week by week, during the terrible wet winter of 1943-44 American and British troops fought inch by inch up the Italian mainland. The heavy rains turned the hillsides into muddy slopes and the troops relied on mules to carry their ammunition and other supplies along tortuous mountain footpaths and tracks as they relentlessly pursued the German divisions who fought over every inch of ground.

To soften up the German resistance the Allied air forces flew missions from their bases in England to attack the industrial towns in the north of Italy. Turin, Milan, Padua and other cities in the still German-occupied north of Italy were prime targets. Not just towns and cities but railway yards, bridges – anything that could stop extra supplies coming from Germany to help the Nazi forces – was a target for the overnight bombers.

However there was a problem. The route to Italy was easily traced on the map. From the many airfields of the flat East Anglian countryside around the famous old English university city of Cambridge and elsewhere the bombers would quickly cross to Holland. Then a short while later they would reach Germany itself and, flying high, they would follow the river Rhine way down below them all the way to the Alps, beyond which lay their Italian targets. But the Alps themselves were mostly in Switzerland, and Switzerland was neutral. Neutral, but with little chance of preventing the bombers flying over their country. Of course they had a few anti-aircraft guns but it was well-known by the Allies that 99 times out of 100 the guns were aimed well below the "targets" at which they were firing: a token resistance. Even so there was always that 100th time and it was to be the misfortune of James's father that he was a navigator on that 100th flight.

With his room-mate at the mess, Luke, in charge of the aircraft, they had taken off from "an airfield somewhere in England", as the radio always described those locations. It was a clear night with a beautiful moon that silhouetted the heavily laden planes as they climbed slowly but powerfully up to their maximum cruising height of 30,000 feet. And soon in a matter of minutes the coast of England was left behind and they could see far below the canals and rivers that criss-crossed the flat Dutch countryside that had already been subjected to Nazi control for the past four years.

Sitting in his navigator's seat, and having eaten a solid meal of steak and eggs before departure, Theo had wondered about those poor people under the enemy yoke. The sooner for everyone this war was ended the better, especially for those folk down there. Maybe one day he would be able to be a tourist and see for himself those funny wooden clog shoes that the Dutch always wore. And the Dutch girls – they looked pretty in their flowery skirts and with those white bonnets that they always seemed to use. That landscape below them appeared in the moonlight to be covered by those ever-turning windmills that he had seen and read about in the National Geographic.

The bombers droned on southwards and then in a short while they knew they were over Germany itself for they could see the wide ribbon of the river Rhine snaking its way through the industrial Ruhr Valley as it flowed down from the Swiss Alps towards the sea. On both sides of their own plane Theo could see the other planes on tonight's mission. Each one a few feet above or below their own so as to make it difficult for any enemy guns below to get a proper range. From time to time Theo spoke over the intercom microphone to the Skipper and gave him a little guidance as they moved on and on ever further from their base back in England. In a short while they would be over the mountainous Alps and then quickly within range of those targets in the industrial cities of northern Italy.

It would be a simple job – fly over the target, get rid of their bombs and quickly back the eight hundred miles to England and land as the dawn broke. He had already completed half a dozen missions to Italy before this one. They only had to blow up bridges and train yards so as to disrupt enemy communications. 'A piece of cake' the Brits called it. Tonight it would be another simple job. A 'simple' job, that was, unless you were on the one hundredth plane…

It was over Switzerland that their trouble started. Four hours out and 600 miles away from those English cooks who had given them such a good meal a few hours back at base, the planes were steadily droning on over southern Germany. Soon they would be past Germany and over neutral Switzerland and so safe for the next 45 minutes. They could then relax slightly and pass round the thermos of hot coffee. Way down below the river Rhine suddenly turned left – to the east – and beyond it lay neutral Switzerland blocking the flight path to Italy. "Blocking" was scarcely the right word for it. Theo had heard all those stories that if the Allied bombers flew high enough then the Swiss guns below seldom managed to reach the planes overhead. Indeed at their pre-flight briefings it was sometimes mentioned that the Swiss deliberately lowered their sights so that the planes were not in danger.

A few weeks before there had been a terrible mistake because as the Rhine turned east it was suddenly no longer the boundary between Germany and Switzerland. A little piece of Swiss territory around the town of Schaffhausen lay to the north of the river. Unfortunately on April 1st 1944 some bombs had been dropped by accident onto that peace-loving land of tinkling cow-bells and alpenhorn-playing yodellers. It had been an accident of navigation but it had naturally upset the Swiss. Quite understandably from time to time the Swiss decided to make their anger known about the incident and the anti-aircraft guns aimed high. The night of Theo's seventh mission was one of those nights.

It was usually quite easy to know when they were over Switzerland because the Swiss left their lights on at night; even the automobiles on the roads could be seen with their headlights glaring and so proclaiming a nation island of peaceful tranquillity amongst a surrounding ocean of war.

At 23.12 Swiss Time Walther Ruston gave the order to fire. A corporal in the Swiss Army by night, and a clerk in a local bank by day, he was in charge of a battery of three anti-aircraft guns situated on the outskirts of his local town. As usual the Swiss searchlights had picked up the aircraft as they had crossed over into their airspace. The US and British pilots usually welcomed these extra lights as almost a guide as to where they were, and which way to go. But not tonight. For a peculiar reason there was, it seemed, almost something menacing in the intensity of the lights from down below them. The way they appeared to dance from one plane to another, and to hold them in their beams for much longer than usual. Two of those lights suddenly flooded the "Mississippi Sue" and were greeted by curses from both Theo and Luke his pilot as they were temporarily blinded and unable to read their instruments.

'What the hell? Why don't they move those damned lights?' came from the skipper. Theo cursed again as one of his rulers dropped to the floor as he went for his dark glasses to overcome the strong lights. To add to the confusion the air around the plane seemed suddenly to be full of red flashes.

'Those bloody Swiss, what do they think they are playing at?' came from up front.

At first Theo himself had been just surprised, then he panicked. Had he guided his skipper back over German territory by mistake? But no, those search lights and guns were firing from that lit-up town below.

'My God,' he thought as the possibility flashed through his mind that perhaps Switzerland had joined in the War, or had been invaded, in the few hours since they had left England.

There was not time to think any more as all of a sudden the aircraft gave a shudder and lurched sideways. The small light that he used to read his cards went out and he grabbed his emergency flashlight.

'Christ!' came the voice of Luke. 'We've been hit.'

Then there was silence except for the comforting continuation of the steady roar of the engines as they disappeared into the welcoming cover of cloud. She was still flying, and maintaining her height. Yet despite the familiar roar of the engines they all knew something was wrong. Hard to describe what, just an eerie something that gnawed at each and every crew member as they sat in their seats. They were all fully aware that below them was the tallest mountain range in Europe, and that those peaks were reaching up to them with snow-capped tops and plunging valleys. It did not need the skipper's voice to come on and tell them there was something amiss and that she was not responding properly to his commands. Everyone had a gut-feeling they were in trouble.

Over the next fifteen minutes there followed a flurry of conversation between pilot and navigator.

'Where are we?'

'Over the Alps.'

'How far to land where we might be able to safely put down?'

'About twenty minutes' flying time.'

'Will it be in Switzerland?'

'No, Italy – occupied Italy.'

There was a long silence, you could almost feel the aircrew hanging on waiting for the skipper to make decisions that were to affect them all, maybe even affect whether they were to live or to die. Then the decision came.

'Theo, take us to the nearest target and we will drop our bombs then try and land. The rest of you prepare to scramble out as soon as we hit the deck. Make for any forest or other cover you can find and try to get to Switzerland. GOOD LUCK!'

The next ten minutes seemed an eternity. The rest of the bombers had disappeared over to the right heading for Milan but they could not move in that direction. Below the little twinkling lights of Switzerland – once so welcome but now the source of danger to their very lives – faded out and were replaced by the Italians and their hostile welcome to the sole enemy aircraft above them above them.

'Bergamo, Skipper,' sang out Theo as he plotted his chart and saw below the glows from half a dozen steam engines in the shunting yards of that important industrial city.

'Get the bombs away!' came the reply from the boss and five tons of high explosives hurtled down upon the assembled freight cars and fussing steam engines below.

Already they were down to 10,000 feet and starting to descend rapidly. The ground below was thankfully flat and with few trees to object to their landing. With one hell of a whoosh they hit the earth in the middle of a wheat field. The wheels below them gave way and there was a sickening thud as the tail-plane spun off. Poor Abe the tail gunner, that would be curtains for him. But there was no time to think about the others. Theo had already removed his parachute, as they were drifting lower and lower, so as to make it easier to evacuate the plane.

'Out! Out! Out!' came the voice of the skipper, although his tone seemed to be struggling more and more as he spoke.

As the bomber hit the ground running the fuselage collapsed and started to break up. A gap appeared on the right hand side of the cockpit and Theo lurched forward towards it. There was a yell from the co-pilot calling for help. Turning his head Theo saw the man, Lars, pulling at the skipper and trying to drag him from his seat. Together they manhandled him through the gap and across a piece of open ground. No sooner had they collapsed exhausted under a small bush when with a mighty roar the fuel tanks exploded and their last link with England and safety was gone.

There was a murmur from the pilot. The eyes of co-pilot and navigator met. As they did so there was a faint low sigh and their skipper entered another world where war was no more and bombing missions unknown. He at least was now beyond all further danger.

Theo gave a low whistle. A whistle that had been pre-arranged in case they were to find themselves all separated under such circumstances but no reply came from the surrounding land. They must get away, and fast, as the possibility of the local militia arriving to investigate the fire and the noise would grow with every minute that passed. Theo's navigating skills came to the fore. Pointing to the moon above and then to the North Star, recognised in the formation of the Plough, he muttered softly to his fellow survivor that they should head north. Switzerland lay to the north and in Switzerland lay safety.

CHAPTER XII

With the Partisans

For the next three days and nights the two slowly and cautiously managed their way north, lying under bushes or in culverts during the day and venturing out at night in search of food whilst kilometre by kilometre working their way in a northwards direction. As dawn approached on the fourth night they lay on the edge of a vineyard gazing down at the picturesque little town of Desenzano. A plume of smoke rose up from a freight train high up on a viaduct. The two men could see it was carrying a load of German tanks presumably on their way to the front lower down the "leg" of Italy.

The town itself was at the bottom end of Lake Garda and local fishermen were out before the sun rose trying to find the odd fish to supplement their wartime food rations. Military patrol boats were already starting their criss-crossing of the lake to ensure only those with military permits were on the water. Lake Garda was not in Switzerland, like one of the other nearby Italian lakes, Maggiore, whose most northerly part was actually over the border. Theo and his fellow survivor from the bomber had wondered whether to head in the direction of that lake but Milan with its military bases lay in the way and in any case the Italian and German border guards would be watching for any escaping allied airmen who might take that route.

On their first night on the ground after the plane crashed the two of them had debated what to do. They had looked at their "survivor escape" maps with which they had been issued for every flight and they had decided that the best way into neutral Switzerland would be from as far north in Italy as possible. Until only some twenty years before that part of Italy had belonged to Austria, itself now part of Germany and they knew that there were still many who were now Italians but who might be still pro-German. So the border with Switzerland might be less well-enforced. It was worth a try.

Meantime from the edge of the vineyard they could see the sun rising on little towns like Salo and Gardone. The old Austrian frontier was only a few miles further up near Limone. But could they get there, and even then? As the sun rose the effect of a lengthy night's walking started to take its toll. The ground was warm, their faces were covered by the overhanging branches of the bushes, and it was not long before the two men were fast asleep. Fast asleep only to be woken by a snuffling noise and the wet tongue of a dog licking Theo's forehead. With a start he opened his eyes and made to reach for his pistol only to hear the words

'Silenzio signor,' in a low tone as his eyes stared into the muzzle of a shotgun carried by an elderly farmer. 'Inglese?' – 'English?'

The question was asked in a low key but with a touch of the conspiratorial. English or American it was not going to make any difference now so Theo slowly nodded.

'E bene, vene.'

The old man beckoned but indicated they should keep bending down as he guided them through the undergrowth, always with his shotgun held casually but at the ready. Some twenty minutes later the little group reached a brick building of the type that they had already seen so often. The red bricks

in the outside wall had lots of gaps – missing bricks – so that
the air could keep the hay inside sweet and not encourage it to
go mouldy. Above it there was a low sloping roof with stones
on the top as if to keep it in place. The old man motioned
them inside holding his fingers to his lips.

'Molti tedeschi' – 'Many Germans'

'Attende, due ore,' – 'Wait, two hours,' he conveyed to them
indicating that he would be back. 'Io trovare i partigiani.'

The word 'partigiani' raised their hopes. These were the
"partisans", the Italians who had already taken up arms against
the Germans and were sabotaging bridges and railway tracks to
slow down German efforts to prevent the progress of the Allies
up the leg of Italy. On the ground these brave men were doing
much the same job as Theo and his crew had been doing from
the air, halting as best they could the trains of ammunitions
and vehicles that were still pouring out of German factories to
the armies of Marshall Kesselring near Rome.

The next two hours passed slowly and always with the fear
that the old man might return with a detachment of enemy
troops or even worse some from the local Gestapo headquarters
in Desenzano. They took turns to stay awake and sure enough
as the sun seemed to be at its highest they saw the old man,
accompanied by a tall man with a limp and large moustache,
walking over the fields toward the barn. To any observing
German patrol that might be nearby the men seemed intent
on discussing the fields of wheat that they were going round.
Every so often they would stop and an animated discussion
would take place with many gesticulations from both of them.
Eventually with a very obvious shrug of his shoulders the old
man indicated he needed a breather and some refreshment for

he took a straw-plaited bottle of red wine out of his haversack and beckoned the other to follow him into the red brick building. As far as all the world was concerned they were going to have their lunch, and doubtless a little siesta.

The two Italians pushed back the old wooden door that was half-hanging on one hinge and entered the building. Theo and his companion stood up.

'Buon giorno, signori.'

The tall man with a limp greeted them and then converting to very passable English asked them, 'You from the aeroplane that come down four days ago?'

They nodded in reply.

'I from i partigiani, I come to take you safe. First you wear these,' he said as he opened his haversack and handed them a mixture of clothes and a couple of hats.

'We go to the mountain,' pointing through a large gap in the wall that served as a window and toward the distant hills bathed in a blue mist. 'I come collect you when the night is dark. I go now, arrivederci.'

He limped off followed by their farmer friend and his ever-faithful dog.

With the clothes the man had given them was a newspaper wrapped round a long loaf of bread with ham slices in between. It was the first real meal they had had since that hearty meal of steak, ham and eggs they had eaten in England. That had been in a different world and in what by now seemed another age. The farmer had also left them his carafe of wine and once again the softness of the hay and the effect of the wine conspired to allow the two escapees to forget their woes for a time.

Soon after night fell, and the same stars appeared in the deep blue black sky as they would later that same evening over far-away New England, there was a low whistle followed by a creak in the poorly-hinged door and their limping friend appeared briefly silhouetted in the frame of the entrance. The two of them were ready and packed, so with little beyond a quick checking glance, they followed him out into the Italian night.

Skirting a couple of vineyards and then passing through an olive grove, the three men set out for the nearby hills on the western side of the lake. Ever-climbing they wended their purposeful way further north. Down below on the moonlit lake they could see the white wake of a paddle steamer making its way over to the little town on the other side of the lake; the town of Sirmione that was dominated by its towering castle. The steamer was a hospital ship and its big red cross appeared as a dark symbol standing out to promote its mission of mercy against the floodlit white of the superstructure.

For two more nights Theo, Lars and their guide worked their way cautiously along the steep wooded sides of the mountains that formed the western edge of Lake Garda. Finally on the third day they were led onto a clearing where three or four dozen rough-looking characters were gathered. These were the fabled "Partisans": The famous Italian partisans, who were their nation's equivalent of the French "maquis".

Operating in small groups, well-armed and with a reputation for giving no quarter to their German foes in vicious skirmishes, these men were held in high regard by the authorities back in the States and in England. Possessing a wide selection of arms as a result of airdrops from the Allies, these men, and sometimes women, moved fast around the countryside in small groups to avoid capture. They made a habit of picking on their foes with a suddenness that had instilled fear in all those who might be the subject of a surprise attack from them. The guide, Eduardo, appeared to be well known to the partisans for he was greeted with a great bear-hug by a small fat man with a black beard. The airmen were introduced and handshakes were made all round. Local red wine – a "bardolino" – was produced together with bread and goats cheese and for a few hours it seemed as if Germany, Hitler and Mussolini did not exist and that the world was at peace. The only thing to spoil it was the way every so often one or two men would get up and wander off to replace those who were standing guard on the perimeter of their little territory on the slopes of that wooded hillside above a most beautiful lake.

As the friendly chatter went on the visitors learned that their guide was normally a peacetime head-waiter in one of the hotels that catered for wealthy Milanese who came out from their city at the weekends to sail their yachts on the lake. The leader of the group, Franco, was a local butcher in Desenzano as had been his father and his grand-father before him. It was not long before the two visitors were being questioned as to their duties in the air force. The partisans often heard the bombers flying overhead in the middle of the night as they were preparing their own efforts for the next day and they were intrigued to learn from where the planes came and what sort of bomb-loads they carried. There was contempt on their faces and the language sounded pretty strong to the two Americans when the guerrillas learnt that the Swiss had shot down the plane.

Theo noticed that when his colleague mentioned that he was also an experienced machine gunner there was an exchange of glances between their guide Eduardo and Franco, the black-bearded leader. Then family stories started to dominate the conversation and whilst in some cases it was all about the latest bambini (Theo wondered about who had fathered them when the men were fighting in the mountains, but it was explained that a little "home leave" was allowed with great care when the Germans were changing units and the new arrivals were not yet familiar with how to police the local residents. The brave men were after all real Italians!) the conversation also showed great concern for ageing parents who daily suffered under the yoke of the invaders.

Franco, who seemed very much in charge of the conversations as well as of the men themselves, gradually steered the talk round to the next morning. They were to attack a German convoy that was due to be coming down the lakeside road heading south to the front. But they had a problem. Their machine gun was sticking, could the brave allied airmen help? The gun was promptly produced and put down with all the great care that indicated how precious this piece of armament was to the courageous men.

Lars was not familiar with the model, it had been made in Czechoslovakia and many of its features were different to anything supplied to the USAF, but at the end of the day a machine gun is a machine gun and after half an hour of being intently watched Lars discovered the fault lay in a pin that had been inserted back to front, hence causing the jamming that was frustrating their new partisan friends.

The next step was not difficult to anticipate. Would the brave allied airmen please join them in striking a blow against the wretched Nazi facisti tomorrow morning? A bridge was to be blown up as a convoy was passing over. The German troops were bound to respond but the partisans would be on the hillside above the road and there was an excellent place for the machine gun and its crew. If the gun was manned by Lars and Theo then there would be two more partisans to deal with the trucks and their guards. The following days they would be safely escorted to the Italian border and then over the hills to Switzerland. Not only would the two allies be heroes but they could be assured that when it was all over, and the war finished, then when Theo and Lars came back on holiday with their families they would be guaranteed the best bottles of Italian wine at their table and they would have the choice of the best meat from the nearby butchers! The two airmen had little choice and the word 'Si' – 'Yes' – came somewhat reluctantly to Theo's lips. Fortunately he did not know enough Italian to add 'with pleasure', and in any case he doubted whether he could have spoken them with conviction.

The plans for the morning were finalised amongst the men and then explained in broken English by Eduardo. Broken English because his former duties as head water at a hotel in Desenzano in time of peace had not included explaining to guests from America and England about angles of fire, hiding in bushes and how to throw hand-grenades downhill at a moving lorry containing troops armed to the teeth.

At four o'clock next morning they were woken from their slumbers and half an hour later were off in single file silently through the dense undergrowth toward the stretch of road

Group of German prisoners-of-war captured by partisans near Brescia, Northern Italy, during the last battle of the war, 30ᵗʰ April 1945.
Photo from the archive of Tullio Ferro

Site of the fighting at Monte Casale
Photo from 'Le colline dei Gonzaga' by Tullio Ferro, ed. Sometti (2004)

between Campione and the nearby town of Limone. According to the information Franco had received from one of the local girls who had been detailed to sleep with a German officer – with any German officer who was passing through and might find his first opportunity when reaching Italy to avail himself of its charms and delights – the convoy was due to set off at 7 am. The partisans needed to be in place an hour earlier.

As the strong beams of the early morning sun rose above the tops of the mountains on the other side of the lake all appeared peaceful and quiet from the vantage point of the machine gun emplacement high above the road. Except for the distant cry of a cockerel welcoming the dawn and the far distant put-put of a small German patrol boat towards the top-end of the lake there was quiet. Quiet that is, unless you were able to spot the slight movement of a small branch here or the scampering away of a small woodland creature there that had suddenly found its mission to find breakfast interrupted by its confrontation with a couple of heavily armed men re-adjusting the sights of their rifles as they peered down at the bridge below. Earlier the two Americans had watched as Franco and another partisan had been carefully burying, under the leaves on the ground, the wire that led to the explosives which they had placed under the arch of that fourteenth-century bridge. A bridge that was destined to end its career of so many centuries at around eight o'clock in the morning on that fine Italian summer's day.

Before long the first signs of the expected convoy were to be seen, or rather to be heard as two motor cycles, each with a soldier holding a light machine gun in the side-car, approached the bridge. Then the convoy proper came round the bend. Each lorry was pulling a field-gun and was followed by a heavily armed escort, the soldiers sitting in the backs of the trucks. The canvas covers had been taken down exposing the metal frames under which the steel helmets of the soldiers appeared as a mass of grey bubbles in the back of the truck. It was as the first escort lorry with its men followed the initial gun over the bridge that Franco pressed the plunger and sixteen men of the Wermacht ended their war on a bright sunny morning by the banks of Lake Garda.

All hell broke out as the following vehicles screeched to a halt and the Germans deployed along the roadside, many falling from the hail of bullets poured into them from the hillside. Theo and Lars played their part raking the ditch by the side of the road from their vantage point above. After ten minutes Theo began to notice that there was more fire coming from those below than from the hill-side. He glanced to the left and saw Franco stand up, his right hand back as he started to lob a grenade down to the road. Suddenly the leader of the partisans twisted his body in a contortion that indicated he would never again serve the best cuts of veal over the counter of his shop when peace was finally restored to the world and the tourists once again came flooding back to sail on the lake and walk the mountain paths.

By now the first of the Germans were starting to advance up the hillside slopes taking advantage of the large boulders that lay amongst the trees and using their superior numbers to support each other with covering fire. It was obviously time to go and they would have to leave the gun behind if they were to move fast. Quickly the two men slithered backwards in the undergrowth before judging it was time to rise to their feet and run. Some of the partisans were lying dead around them as they set off fast. For a moment Theo had a glimpse of their old friend the guide with a limp. He was propped up against the trunk of a tree with a small dribble of blood still oozing from the corner of his mouth. Nor would any future tourists ever benefit from his cheerful voice welcoming them to their tables and enquiring if they had had a nice day on the Lake before suggesting they might try a bottle of Bardolino to go with their veal. Those days would not return in a hurry; but "hurry" was the word and Theo set off at a pace.

They had run for perhaps twenty minutes dodging between trees and round rocky outcrops when all of a sudden Lars grabbed out at a tree branch to stop himself, causing Theo to almost fall over him. Lars pointed. Ahead was a tangle of barbed wire and behind it every so often a post with a notice bearing the two words, 'Halten, Minen.' – 'Beware, Mines.' They had reached their limits, they could go no further. Behind them they could hear the voices of the German platoon which was following them. They turned, their war was finally up. They were, as the Brits would say, "in the bag".

CHAPTER XIII

A war by any other name

Monday, September 11th 2006. Another fine day dawned just as it had exactly five years ago in Manhattan. And so it did that that morning at the hotel in the northern Italian resort on the south shore of Lake Garda.

Christina had not wanted to be in New York City five years on from that eventful morning. President George Bush and the First Lady, Laura Bush, would be at Ground Zero but Christina knew that she just could not face being there, nor did she want her seven-year-old George and his little sister Maria to be there.

Besides there was a new baby half-brother, William, born four years after the fateful 9/11. Miracles could happen; for in a different way Christina had found happiness with her new husband, Noah. She had met him at a parents' meeting for the school that George was attending. Noah had lost his own wife in the same building on the same dreadful morning. He had shown Christina a picture of her. African-American and originally from Aruba in the Dutch Antilles, she was a tall, good-looking girl. There had been a child on the way, Noah had said, but its fate was never to be born.

Soon after Christina and Noah had met he had taken her to his old family home at Newport, Rhode Island and had shown her round. Noah had driven her firstly to visit "Breakers". Now owned by the Preservation Society of Newport it was formerly the summer-house of the Vanderbilt family. Whilst in the line to enter the house he explained that like so many of Newport's old houses it had originally been of wood but had been destroyed in a fire just before the Christmas of 1892. What they now saw before them was a magnificent "new" grey-stone building three storeys high – and said to be fireproofed. Later they walked down to Market Square and saw the site where the old ferry used to dock from Jamestown. This had been the main link on the way to the mainland until the building of the new bridge in 1969. Much of the rest of the day was passed on the Newport Beach with its gently sloping fine sands running down to the water's edge. Not long after that visit Christina found that she was pregnant and a wedding was quickly arranged at one of the churches in New York City, with a reception at a nearby East End restaurant on Lexington Avenue.

The two of them had decided that each wanted to remember five years on from 9/11 in their own ways. So when James and Helen had offered to take Christina over to Europe and to visit some of the sights where James' own father Theo had been during the time he was there half a century ago the adults had all decided to go together. Europe would be a lovely place to get away from all the hassle and talk of terrorism and war.

Christina had arranged for one of her friends to have little George and Maria as well as baby William to stay with her own children at the friend's vacation home in Maine. Her nanny would go along to help with Christina's youngsters. Once all this was organised the plans for the European trip had gone ahead.

Through all the post 9/11 traumas Helen and James had been a great support to Christina and they had taken to Noah with no ill-feeling or rancour. He was a new father to their own grandchildren and anyway Christina was still young so it was their duty to support her in every way. A perceptive and intelligent man, James had realised that five years on would be a difficult time. If his daughter-in-law could get through such a commemorative date then she would be able to stride forward into the future. It was rather like a hurdler at the Olympics. It was not the first hurdle that was the really critical one, but rather that after it there were a couple that had been taken in the runner's stride. Once they had been achieved, there would be that confidence to carry on for the rest of the race.

James took to organising the European venture with gusto. They would fly to London, spend a few days looking up old family places in England and then travel by train to Italy. If they could be in Italy on 11th September they, together with Noah, could find something to occupy Christina on that particular day. The fall in Europe would be so different to that at home.

It was whilst waiting at the line-up at JFK for the American Airlines flight that they noticed a change in the atmosphere in the terminal. The line was taking much longer than usual to shuffle forward and there seemed to be almost a hush spreading over the building. Eventually rumours started to filter through the crowds at the different gates. Someone said that there had been another terrorist attempt on an airline. Then, 'No, it was a scare but not an attack.' People started to look around them and to talk in low tones. One mother with a babe in her arms and another little one at her feet stepped out of the line and appeared to be saying to a ground hostess that she had decided not to fly. They were escorted back through Security. James and Helen exchanged glances. Christina had her eyes fixed to the floor around her feet.

Eventually an official came down the line explaining that the Brits had discovered a possible plot but that nothing had actually happened and their flight would go ahead, although with extra security it might be delayed. James turned to his daughter-in-law.

'We think you should decide, my dear. Do you still want to fly today?' he asked in a kindly voice.

Christina took a long breath.

'If we let them win,' she said, her face the colour of chalk and with a tremor in every syllable, 'then there is no future for my children. Let's carry on and fly.'

Taking that decision, standing in a line at JFK, was one of the most difficult Christina had taken since Noah had asked her to marry him. It would have been so easy to say 'no' and to return home to Manhattan but that would have meant giving way. It would have meant that for ever in the future she had accepted defeat at the hands of OBL and his crowd. They had torn her life to pieces once and she had put it together again albeit still in a very fragile condition; but to step out of that line now and get a cab back to town was accepting defeat. She would in the future always know that she had been defeated by those evil men and women. She owed it to George and Maria to carry on. Their great grandfather Theo had stood up for freedom and they were going to Italy to honour him. She would not be defeated in her turn. She was not prepared in the future to have to admit to the children that she had been defeated by the same people who had killed their father.

In her handbag she had a small plastic bag that was always with her wherever she went. It contained some grains of dust from the site of Ground Zero. It had been given to her by someone involved in the clearance and she liked to think that perhaps, just perhaps, those grains of grey dust might include the smallest and tiniest remains of her beloved Robert. If anything happened today over the Atlantic then they would be together – into eternity.

So many things had either changed or come and gone during those five years. Her life, those of her children, and of course the lives of James and Helen who had lost such a wonderful son. Not only was it their family life which had been swallowed up by that terrible all-enveloping darkness but so had the world. Twice, within living memory of some even in that terminal today, Americans had come together as a nation and saved the world. In 1917 under President Wilson and again in 1941 after Pearl Harbor and under the leadership of FDR, America had led the world to victory over evil. Now a new president, George W. Bush, had told Congress and the rest of the world to beware of an "axis of evil" and he had led the nations into another coalition, or so it all seemed to Christina. Her wonderful Robert had been as much a victim of evil on September 11th 2001 as had been those brave Navy boys on their ships at Pearl Harbor in December 1941.

With such thoughts in her mind the long-caring fingers of sleep closed about Christina as the Boeing left New England far below, passed the broad mouth of Canada's St Lawrence River some 35,000 feet underneath them, and headed out over the North Atlantic to Great Britain. She had Noah beside her and the children were safe back in Maine.

Two seats away, with his long legs stretched out into the aisle, James was also wondering about the earth below them, and its future. An intellectual by nature and an academic by training he was much less sure than his daughter-in-law about the direction this president and Congress were taking their nation and the world.

James remembered how his father had been in Italy with the partisans when he himself was being born. It would have needed just one stray bullet from a German rifle – or even from what these days was euphemistically called "friendly fire" – and James would never have known his father. Thankfully it had not happened; but they had lost their Robert. He had lost that son – who had as a baby bounced gleefully on James' knees; that seven year old child who had clung to his neck one day when out sailing in Narragansett Bay when a sudden wind had struck up, that same son who had proudly introduced his parents to a new girlfriend and some years later had excitedly called from the hospital in Manhattan to say a new generation of their family had arrived and must be entered into the Jackson family bible. The loss of such a fine son as Robert was still at times almost too much to bear.

And now this new president was talking of another war. A war that seemed to be destined to last for many years into the future. Would little George back there at home be the victim one day of this new war? The thought was too much to imagine.

James closed his eyes. His wife, and beyond her Christina, were both fast asleep. Christina had her head resting on Noah's shoulder and that in itself told James how right they had been to encourage her when one evening she had asked for their blessing as she was about to marry again. Yet that night, as the plane flew through the darkened world, James could not sleep. The earth lay below him, his fellow passengers around either slumbered, watched a movie or stayed slaves to their personal electronic gadgetry. But to James it was as if he was in a capsule of history some six miles high above a world that was tearing itself apart yet again.

As with many Americans, James had been brought up with a vision of two worlds. A "They" and an "Us". A "New World" and an "Old World". Rich and poor nations; and within his own country rich and poor folk. As had many who lived in his "New World" of the USA he was still very conscious of his "Old World" roots. His own grandfather, Leonard, had sometimes told him of how his grandparents, another Robert and Caroline, had made their long arduous journey to settle in New York City. It had taken them weeks in a sailing ship to make, in the opposite direction, a journey that would take tonight's flight only a matter of seven hours. Robert and Caroline had made that voyage seeking economic and social freedom and prosperity in the New York of the 1850s. They had bought the American Dream of their generation and had helped to create the great American way of life. Was that way now in jeopardy?

Thinking about it, it almost seemed as if in a way his son Robert had died for their sake. He had been creating prosperity in his financial world; and freedom flowed from prosperity. So why did some in the "Old World" want to terrorise and even destroy that freedom?

Was it the fault of religious fanatics? Was it because some were jealous of the success of others? Or could it – just possibly – be that the American nation had brought much of the problem upon itself? Most US citizens of course could not possibly contemplate that they were in any way at fault and so the cause of today's woes.

But the academic in his training had taught James that most products were the result of the synthesis, the coming together, of different strands. Like life itself attitudes, opinions and factsall had DNA-like components. Just as each of we humans might carry within us unpleasant harbingers of the future or wicked thoughts in our psyche, so a nation must be expected to have within its make-up elements that it did not want or which might be life-threatening. So could his own great USA possibly have brought some of the present situation upon itself?

This President – someone whom as a New England Democrat James did not like – had called it "the war on terror". Sure there was a war going on in Iraq, in Afghanistan, and elsewhere. But was there a hidden war – a war by any other name – that was raging around the American (call it "western" if you like) way of life in the hearts and minds of ordinary folk all over the world? A hidden war of attitudes and beliefs?

By now most about him on the plane were asleep; a hostess was padding silently around offering plastic mugs of water to those few still awake. James took a proffered cup and let the lukewarm, yet still refreshing, water trickle down his throat. He marvelled at how the girl managed, despite what must be her own personal fears within her on the flight, to look so calm and even to smile when she received a grateful 'thank you' for the clear liquid. Somehow her beautifully pronounced murmur 'you're welcome' seemed to personify all that was good about the US way of life. How could anyone take objection to American ways of behaviour? And yet the thought of whether some of this frightening crisis might be home-reared nagged at him. As a fifth-generation American, could even he be partly responsible? It would be something to ponder on when they were safely – if they were safely – in that Old World where so many folk and beliefs had their roots.

James closed his eyes as the 767 crossed the point in mid-Atlantic where the New World gave way to the Old.

CHAPTER XIV

Back to the Old World

Next morning at London's Heathrow Airport they were all made very much aware of their arrival in a different world. The long line-ups at Immigration were something to see. There seemed to be two "queues" as the Brits quaintly called them. Back home as an American citizen they were used to walking through into the country quite quickly, even these days. But here in London they were made to join a "queue" consisting of people of all colours and creeds and arriving from all over the world. At home of course you could always hear a multitude of languages and accents but in London it was the different styles of dress that struck one. Arab men with their veiled women in tow, African men in flowing multi-coloured long robes. Australians in bush-hats, neatly tailored Japanese businessmen and their co-patriot small slim young women in tight Levis or wearing the latest styles from the western world. The whole world seemed, that early morning, to be arriving in London, England.

What struck James above all was that only American voices could be heard in the line-ups. All the rest appeared to be patiently and quietly waiting to step forward and show their passports and visas. Yet from wherever two or more Americans were standing together could be heard loud exchanges or opinions on their flight itself, on the food, or even from where had each come from back home and where they were heading to now they were on European soil. Americans did stand out in a crowd.

James fell silent. Beside him Helen and Christina were discussing whether Maria was now ready for school and if she would fit in with her peers. They were speaking loudly and to him perfectly normally. But James could see on the faces of those behind a mixture of resignation and annoyance that their own private thoughts were being disrupted by the volume of conversation between his wife and his daughter-in-law. In all their innocence were those closest to him making their unknown contributions to that "war by any other name"?

London was not a place to be that August weekend. The city was swarming with armed police and there was a feeling that anything might happen at any time. It seemed very reminiscent of Manhattan in the days that followed 9/11, except nothing had actually happened. TV and press were full of reports about plots to blow up as many as 12 planes mid-Atlantic.

It had always been part of their plans to move out of town and to go to the north of England to see where Robert and Caroline had come from those 150 years ago. James hoped that the trip would relieve the tension which he could see on the faces of both his womenfolk. On Christina's image that tension was evident at every corner of her eyes and her mouth. So renting a car from Hertz all four of them set off on the Monday morning. First they made for Shakespeare's country and the little market town of Stratford-upon-Avon. Noah, who had bought a guide book along, told them the "Avon" was the local river and that they were in the shire of Warwick, but the English did not call it "War wick" as the town in Rhode Island was called. Instead these Brits said "Warrick". How very odd. The old buildings seemed familiar from when he and Helen had visited the place years ago, but the town was much busier and they found it difficult to park the car.

Later they they set off for the north of England and reached Stonefield where they stayed the night at an old English inn. The black and white timber-framed building stood in the market square of the very town from which Robert and Caroline had left for America one and a half centuries before.

Each of these English "inns" seemed to be called after some person – often a king or queen or other historical notable. But why ever would you call an inn "The Dog and Duck" or "The Frog"? He was beginning to understand why his ancestors had left the "Old World".

He and Helen had a reasonably sized room with a "four poster" bed – but a mattress that must have been made at the same time as Shakespeare had been writing "Hamlet" perhaps back in Stratford! There were dark brown wooden beams in the ceiling and a sloping floor. However James felt that they were lucky that they had their own bathroom. Not all inns were that modern and he remembered once reading how before the water-closet was invented it had been common to empty the chamber pots out of the window onto the streets below – and on any passing pedestrian! England, he was glad to note, had moved with the times to some extent!

In the evening they dined in an oak-panelled room where judging by the colours of the wood the trees must have been cut down about the same time as those used for the building of the "Mayflower". Although it was still late summer a log fire blazed in an open hearth throwing its flickering reflections up onto the old wooden beams of the low ceiling. Beside the fireplace stood an ancient grandfather clock which chimed every half hour and on the face of which were written the name of the makers, the town where it had been made and the date 1790. That was the year Rhode Island had joined the Union as the thirteenth state! Had that venerable old timepiece been standing there, watching over generations of diners, ever since? Tonight they were really back in history!

After the meal they adjourned into the bar and James cast his eye over the locals sitting in groups at tables. Each seemed to have a large beer in front of him. Some had their beer in glasses of varying shapes whilst some had tankards made of glass or pewter. It seemed that every local had his particular drinking vessel and when a new arrival walked in the door the barman seemed to have reached for his special container and filled it to its frothing limit even before the newcomer had crossed the floor and reached the long brown bar with its arrangement of taps and levers. Somewhere in the back of James' mind he could remember someone mentioning these features of English bars to him once before, but who was it? Then through the years and deep mists of the past he remembered Robert, their beloved Robert, making comments about English pubs after he had been over from Stateside on his first business trip to London all those years ago. A tiny tear crept into James's left eye but he brushed it away before it was spotted by the others.

In one corner of the bar a group were playing darts but their beers were never far away. As every beer was consumed it was refilled as if automatically, never a word was spoken and James never spotted money changing hands until someone got up to go home.

What talk there was, was in low tones and it seemed to all be about the TV news and the spectre of terrorism. Yet for these good folk London, let alone Manhattan, must seem a long way away. They were places probably most if not all had never visited and had only seen on TV.

Maybe this was why the discussions were so low-key and there seemed to be a blanket of calmness lying over the room with its ancient timbered features. Or maybe it was those old beams above their heads in the bar that gave rise to the calm, James reflected. Those same beams had held that ceiling together when news had reached England of victory over the French fleet by the English admiral Nelson in 1805. The same beams had heard the news of the defeat of Napoleon in 1815 and of Germany twice in 1918 and 1945. On each of these occasions those tankards must have been raised to celebrate success over the enemy. But had all those pewter tankards stayed fast to the tables when news arrived of the surrender of the British to the Americans at Yorktown and the end of the War of Independence (or "the American Revolution" as the Brits called it?) Maybe it was this feeling that wars could come and go which had caused the differences between the USA and its old colonial masters who were now its closest ally.

And perhaps this was why all these English folk talked so calmly and quietly. They had seen all those things before and in any case as James knew there had not been an invasion of England for nearly a thousand years. Even their own Civil War over here had been more than two hundred years before Gettysburg. This country had seen all these things time and time again and the word "war" must be part of their vocabulary. Would, James wondered, America ever become like this? And if so when Americans had learned over the centuries to absorb tragedies and crises, would future line-ups at airports be much quieter? Would the world ever reach that far?

The next few days in Britain were fascinating. All the talk was of the threat of terrorism, but what seemed to interest most people was the fact that it had apparently been a "home grown" plot by young Muslims who had been born and bred in England. Young Muslims whose parents had come to Britain to make a new and better life.

In that old North-of-England market town of Stonefield, the very area from where Robert and Caroline had left back in the 1850s, many of the old factories had disappeared. Just as at home in New England the textile industry, cotton spinning and wool weaving, had either disappeared or become reduced to the odd factory. Sometimes one could still come upon large redbrick buildings with in one corner a square tower for the stairs between the floors and a tall round chimney. It was rather like the situation back home in New England where many of the old textile factories had been converted to modern light industry with perhaps a dozen micro-industries in the same building; whilst others were standing forlorn and empty in some out of the way New Hampshire or Rhode Island small town. Ghosts of an industrial past.

Even so in the ancient Stonefield it was still possible to walk the same streets where great-great grandfather Robert had once walked to market with that wholesome lass who later had both shared all his joys and sorrows, and the adventures of settling in a new land. Of course the shop fronts were all modern but if one looked up above street level the facades of many old buildings must have looked much the same in the 1850s before his family had set off to sail to New York. The funny thing was that the centres of the English towns were almost always only of two levels and it was only now and again that they would be much taller. It was as if only at the ground-level had the buildings progressed into the twenty-first century.

There was a pub, as it was called in England, in the "High" street where they all went in for lunch. That warm beer again! Even Noah was beginning to accept it, if not quite to like it. Somehow it just seemed to fit the atmosphere. Of course the food was good and it was always easy to start a conversation with the Brits – but why did they always call chips 'crisps' and french fries 'chips'?

'Ah! Thee be from Amerikee?' came from an old man in a corner seat near to them. A cloth cap had been pulled down over his bald head until it nearly touched the tip of the pint-glass in front of him when he drank. The question seemed to slip out of the gap between his cap and the glass.

'I knowee accent, we had sum of ee here during the war.'

James was tempted to ask, 'Which war, against Hitler, the Kaiser or perhaps even Napoleon?' Instead he contented himself with 'Yes, sir. We are from New England,' wondering what would come next in the conversation. Terrorism? The temperature of the beer? Perhaps the latest news from the White House or from Iraq?

'Oi thought theer be only wun England, that be enough for me!' slipped out just before half-way was reached in the glass. It was followed by a sleeve reaching up and wiping the beer-froth from the lips of the old man.

'Well sir,' James could see the conversation was going in an unexpected direction, 'we also have a "New" England over back home.' He paused.

'But of course you have the original one here. We also have a New York,' he added, 'and that is called after your city York I believe.'

Two beady eyes gave a flash that amounted to a quizzical look of interrogation.

'York be full of furriners. They be called Yorkshire-men but they b'aint be no good at cricket.'

James could see he was entering dangerous waters and he seemed to be adventuring onto tribal territory. It was like saying to a fan of the Texas Rangers that the Yankees and New York were the centre of the sporting world. The ancient city of York, James knew, was the other side of the Pennine Hills that divided the east from the west of England; but as to who was the better at cricket – well how did they play cricket anyway? Somebody had once described it to him after a visit to England as "the poor man's baseball". The talk really did seem to be going nowhere and it was saved by the arrival of steak and french fries, sorry 'chips'.

'Moi dad wunce told me oi got cussins in Amerikee,' came out of the corner as they later had their cappuccinos. 'Wunder if you knows them?' The interrogation had started again.

'Me great grandfather and his sister, they went there from here sumtime middle of sentry 'fore last.'

James glanced at Noah as if asking him to try and get the subject changed, but before he could do so the next statement that escaped between the pint of Stonefield Bitter and the toothless lips sent them into stunned silence.

'Name of Jackson. Ever heard of them? Summ't to do with railways me old dad used to say.'

Helen had great difficulty lowering her half-empty cappuccino onto the saucer without it spilling over onto the table.

James took a deep breath. He needed that oxygen to get into his brain before he could respond. It was Noah who came to the rescue.

'I know one or two Jacksons back home,' he said with a warning glance at Christina. 'Do you happen to know what they were called?'

'Sem as me oi guess, me name's Rabbert. Think as how that was wat me ol grandpa used to say.'

Sensing that this might become a little embarrassing all ways round and take up all their time whilst in the town, Noah looked over to James and observed the fleetest shake of the head.

'Well sir, if I meet any of them when we get back home I will mention it to them, but we must be going. So nice to meet you sir.'

The four of them rose to their feet and headed for the door. As they passed the bar tender James gently slid a ten pound note over the counter with a quiet 'let him have a couple more on us please' and then they were outside. Were they right? Would they regret for the rest of their lives not developing that conversation? But they had to get on and were due to drive over to Chester that afternoon.

They had booked in at the Grosvenor Hotel and wanted to see those city walls shown in the brochures. City walls for what purpose? To keep out American tourists? They hoped not.

CHAPTER XV

Over The Channel

A few days later the four of them set off to leave England and to head for Italy and to see the places where Theo had spent his time more than 50 years ago. The old man was now suffering from Alzheimer's and in a home just outside New Haven. He would not be able to understand their tales of the visit to Europe when they got back but there was a sense of duty that took them on this pilgrimage. It was exactly sixty years – more than half a century – since the old veteran had arrived back Stateside after being freed from incarceration at the end of the war.

"The War" it used to be called, then later it had become "The Last War" so what was this new "war on terrorism" to be named by history? Would it even be on the same scale? James prayed to heaven that it would not and that none of the next generation would suffer as had Theo and his compatriots.

Avoiding the centre of London they drove down to Dover, the port near which the Channel Tunnel would take them to France. Last time he and Helen were there they had gone by passenger train from London to Paris with the train going through that same tunnel. This time they were to take the car on the train.

For an American it was always confusing. You hired a car in England and with the steering column on the right hand side but you drove on the left of the road until you left England. Then once in Europe-proper you drove on the right hand side of the road, as at home, but of course the steering wheel was still on the right as well, which made it even more difficult. No wonder most from home flew everywhere when they were over here. It made overtaking somewhat hazardous and it also did not help that the English hire car speedometer was in miles per hour but the speed limits in France and elsewhere were all in kilometres per hour.

They arrived at Dover before lunch and as their booking reservation for the train from nearby Folkestone was not until later in the day they decided to look around the town. The busy harbour was full of ferries coming and going between that port and France only 20-something miles away. It was a clear day and when they drove up onto the high Dover cliffs above the town they could see similar white chalk cliffs over in France as those that lay beneath their feet when still in England.

There was time for them to visit the castle on those cliffs. It had been built by the last real invader of England, the French "William the Conqueror" who had claimed the English kingship in 1066. Ever since, that castle and those white cliffs of Dover, had been symbols of English defiance of all that was dominant the other side of the English Channel. It was there that Prime Minister Churchill had stood, looking across that narrow strip of water over to France; just as over the other side Herr Hitler had looked over at England before finally deciding not to try and copy that William as another would-be conqueror of England. It must have been from those white French – then called Gaul – cliffs that Julius Caesar had contemplated the invasion of England. There was no escaping history in this country. Maybe his own father had seen the cliffs when he flew over the Channel to bomb Italy on that fateful night in 1944?

In the soft chalk under the ancient castle the English had first dug tunnels over 200 years ago so as to defend themselves against another threatened French invasion, one by Napoleon Bonaparte. Then during Theo's time more tunnels had been dug and it was possible to take a tour seeing the rooms that had been used as radio quarters, barracks and so many other things in preparation for resisting the forces of Nazism. As they went on the tour round those tunnels with a guide James could not help feeling there were one or two places that were not open to the public and perhaps secret plans for defence were once again being put together. With all these threats in the modern world were the sands starting to run out for the Brits once more?

It was Christina's turn to drive and she carefully manoeuvred the automobile onto the covered train wagon that was to take them under the sea to France. Once a route so heavily fought over for two thousand years it was now a tourist route and one could only wonder what rotting hulks of old wooden sailing ships or rusting remains of more modern battleships were above them as they sped along in their train. They had the choice either to sit in the car or stand outside its doors. From time to time security personnel passed up and down the whole length of the train but the journey was only under half an hour and then they were able to drive straight off onto the French expressway and head south.

By 5pm they were all tired of travelling. Reaching a small French town they enquired at the local tourist office for overnight accommodation. A helpful young lady told them of an apartment rented out at a small French farm nearby and just off the main road. Having booked in they sought out a local restaurant and enjoyed their first experience on the holiday of exquisite French cuisine. Later back at the farm they all four relaxed over a bottle of the local "vin ordinaire" produced for them by the kind farmer's wife.

So far it had been a thought-provoking drive. They were close to the border with next-door Belgium. It was along this route that had lain the front line in the First World War where General Pershing and his boys had come to support the Allies. Germany had quickly and successfully invaded Belgium in 1914 and then after intensive fighting the line had stabilised for a distance of some 600 miles right down to the frontier of neutral Switzerland. For four years there had been bloody combat with attacks and counter attacks but little territory was taken or given on either side. Yet what had been given were the lives of the youth of all the countries involved in that bloody stalemate across the rolling French fields of the old province of Flanders and beyond.

These, happily, were more peaceful days for France and even the talk of terrorism seemed to have vanished by comparison with when they had been in England. Or so it seemed to them all until James gently pointed out that perhaps it was because all the newspapers were in French rather than English that they had not noticed things quite so much.

The following night they stopped in a small hotel in a beautiful little town set amongst the Vosges mountains of eastern France and overlooking the River Rhine that was the modern frontier with Germany. They were, of course, still in France but the village where they were staying, and most of the other places around, had German-sounding names. Checking in Noah's guide-book they learned that the area had for many years been part of nearby Germany and the border had moved to and fro according to who had won the latest war. These Europeans really were incredible with their old history. But whoever owned the land over the years the locals had obviously learned how to make an excellent local white wine. James made a note that when back home he would ask his local wine merchant whether they could get him some Gewürztraminer.

After breakfast it was a quick drive of just over an hour before they arrived in Switzerland near the major industrial city of Basel. Wanting to get on they pressed forward and by lunch they had their first view of the Alps. The whole country seemed to be split between north and south by this range of snow-covered mountains stretching up into the blue sky. Beyond lay Italy and somehow those mountains had to be crossed to get there.

It was a lovely old building in which they stopped that night. It was built of wood which appeared to have been stained a dark brown either with the local varnish or simply from age. The low roof jutted out well over the edge of the building and was intricately carved whilst the flag outside showed a big bear. The language spoken was German but the reliable old guide-book told them that German was only one of four languages that were official despite it being such a small country. Everywhere they went it seemed as if all the houses, and even the small little shops and restaurants, had a box of red geraniums at every window. These, and the wooden houses with their overhanging roofs, looked as if they had been copied straight from the cover of a box of chocolates.

There was an atmosphere of quietness and efficiency everywhere. Even the grass verges along the road sides had been cut to gather in the hay so as to feed the cattle in winter when the land was covered by snow. But it was the cattle themselves in Switzerland that were such a surprise. They were not the medium-sized black and white cows they had seen elsewhere in Europe. Those black and whites always looked as if they were specially bred to produce semi-skimmed milk but these Swiss beasts were mostly a reddish-brown. They were larger and stood on four sturdy legs that seemed ideal to carry their own weight and probably also the rich milk that was used in the country's famous chocolate bars. But it was the noise that was fascinating, for each individual cow had a large bronze bell hanging round its neck and as the animals moved about the fields munching the grass the bells clanged continually. It was literally as if the hills were alive with music that gave a charm of its own to the nation.

A clear blue sky served as a backdrop to the snow-covered peaks that seemed to stretch from the horizon on the left to the horizon on the right as next morning they set off to cross the Alps with the aim of reaching their hotel in Italy that night. That range of high mountains stood in their way just as they had done for centuries and yet somehow mankind had always found a way through them. One early general, Hannibal, had actually taken his troops through the snows accompanied by his personal weapon of mass destruction, a herd of elephants! Napoleon had marched through the passes on his way to invade Italy and in more recent times it was common for adventurous travellers to cross by "diligence", a European version of what James and Helen would call a "stagecoach".

189

But all those epic crossings of the Alps were isolated incidents. Modern times had introduced railways and later expressways as means of travelling from north to south and vice versa. No longer would the intrepid individual try to cross the Great St Bernard Pass high up and knee-deep in snow with the comforting knowledge that the monks at the top kept specially trained dogs with small barrels of brandy around their necks. Those barrels had been to succour the exhausted walkers who chose to cross the hard way and maybe then got lost in that snow.

Having looked at the maps the night before and studied the alternative ways of crossing the mountain barrier, Christina, Noah and her parents had chosen to go via the St Gotthard Pass. This involved at one stage transferring the car onto an open rail wagon so that they could avoid either the steep passes with hairpin bends or the fast modern auto-routes that seemed full of commercial trucks going in both directions. It seemed strange sitting in their car and being in a tunnel thousands of feet below the surface of the earth yet hurtling along as the fast electric locomotive made easy work of the auto-wagons behind it. James mused to himself whether this was what hell was like for those who found their way there after being refused entry through the pearly gates of heaven by St Peter? Probably not, as it was quite cold sitting in their car with just the frequent on-off illumination of the tunnel lights as each flashed past.

All of a sudden they were out into the sunshine, and what a difference! The grey skies from north of the Alps had all magically given way to a warmth that seemed to reach into their very bones. Not only was it warmer but the whole picture before them seemed more mellow. There was a softer light as if they had entered a new world that was welcoming them with open arms and giving them a hug. The train slowed down and then they were off onto the roads. They were still in Switzerland but this was a different Switzerland. One where all the names of the little villages were in Italian, the third (amongst equals) language of that spectacular country. Even the buildings were different. The brown sloping roofs of the north, built to hold the snow in winter and keep the wooden houses warm, had given way to more frequent flat roofs of square stuccoed brick buildings often painted in white or cream. Obviously they did not have the amounts of snow that there were further north so the need to keep the houses warm with a thick layer of snow on the roof all winter was no longer a requirement. The odd field of vines started to appear at the roadside and it seemed that in no time they were entering the bustling city of Lugano.

Parking their car amongst many others on a tree-lined boulevard they set off to explore the city. Helen was worried about all their valises and everything else being left in such a public place but James assured her that as this was Switzerland, there was a code of mutual respect amongst the citizenry and no one would think of breaking into their vehicle.

In the warm relaxing atmosphere of this lovely lakeside town it was natural that Christina slipped her arm round Noah's waist as they walked down to the water's edge. It was their first view of one of the "Italian" lakes. Although they were still in Switzerland the whole atmosphere seemed different to that part of the country north of the Alps. Somehow everything seemed "Italian". The language in the shops, the wording on the signposts, even the sky seemed a different more "cosy"

and gentle welcoming blue. On the lake were dotted pleasure
steamers and private boats of various shapes and sizes, some
with motors and some with sails. It was a glorious sight.

They all bought ice cream from a stand along the esplanade
then meandered amongst the exotic flowers in the little gardens
that separated the lakeside promenade from the busy road that
ran along the side of the lake. The four of them paused for
a few charming minutes outside one large restaurant where a
small orchestra was playing for the guests an enchanting tune
that sounded vaguely familiar to Christina.

'What is that tune called?' she asked James.

'Volare' came his reply.

At once Christina was transported back to another world.
How many years ago was it since she last heard that tune? It
was on their trip to Paris. They were newly married and at a
cabaret in Montmartre, the "naughty" part of Paris. They had
gone on a tourist-organised night out that the concierge at their
hotel had recommended. First the coach had taken the party
– a dozen or so American couples together with a sprinkling
of Norwegians, Danes and Dutch as well as one British couple
– to a cellar near the Eiffel Tower where a performer had
demonstrated the swallowing of a whole series of razor blades
without even once cutting himself. Then they had moved to
a small theatre where a French comedian was performing.
The French audience had seemed to enjoy it but the language
was a definite barrier for the Americans and others. Finally
they had all landed up at a cabaret in Montmartre. There on-
stage nudity, or ninety-nine percent such, was obviously the
"dress of the day" with a series of musical and dance acts that
gradually increased in volume and daring. "Volare" had been

one of the tunes being repeated over and over again with the audience joining in.

By time they had left and the coach driver had got them safely back to their hotel in the early hours only one subject had been in the minds of both Christina and Robert. She had purchased earlier that day in a big store a very inviting negligée set and once in their room it had not taken long for her to invite Robert to pay it close attention. They had even gently hummed "Volare" together as they made love that night.

But that now seemed so long ago and here she was hearing the same haunting tune with her new husband Noah. As she stood at the lakeside looking over to the mountains on the other side she secretly made a vow to herself that tonight she would give Noah a "Volare experience" that he would remember for a long time to come.

'Come on, Dream Lady!'

She was suddenly conscious of James looking wistfully at her. He knew his daughter-in-law and could often read her thoughts to a degree. He knew something was stirring inside her and guessed that it might be a ghost from the past.

'Come on, let's all go and have some lunch,' he said gently holding her shoulder and steering her away towards a road crossing. 'We will have something to eat and then you two women can go and do a spot of Swiss-shopping here in Lugano whilst Noah and I look around that church over there and perhaps take a stroll.'

They sat at a small table with a red and white chequered tablecloth in an open square. They all had pizzas washed down with soft drinks and followed by coffee. Helen could not resist the "complimentary" bowl of red cherries that was in the centre of the table whilst James suspected that, Switzerland being Switzerland, the cherries would appear on the final bill in a somewhat disguised form. The Swiss were always keen business-folk.

Their cappuccinos finished, and the last few cherries looking very lonely by themselves, Helen and Christina then set off on their shopping expedition. They meandered under the arcades that held behind them many small shops. Small they might be but the window displays, which needed lighting because the thick walls of the arches excluded the strong daylight and brought down the excessive heat outside to a comfortable warmth, were most inviting. Every shop seemed to be beckoning you in. You really had to buy that cashmere scarf or that leather handbag. How could a girl resist them? But the prices were not cheap by any means.

They paused outside one shop and Helen saw a gleam in Christina's eyes. This, her mother-in-law decided, was one time where discretion was the better part.

'I just want to look at those calendars over there,' she said, leaving her daughter-in-law to enter the best display of lingerie she had seen since she had visited Victoria's Secret just before they left New York.

Meantime the two men had wandered off on their own. Their first port of call was the church but they found it too ornate for their liking so in no time they walked back down to the lakeside and stretched their legs for nearly thirty minutes. The lake steamers were fascinating. They had expected to see paddle-steamers perhaps with back funnels as they had on the Swiss lakes north of the Alps but these were all motorised vessels. One boat-full of tourists was crossing the lake to a small village on the far side. On asking a local postcard vendor to where it was sailing they were told that it was crossing to Campione, a settlement that was Italian territory but surrounded by Switzerland. There was a casino there and it was a popular day trip, especially on a Sunday, for the local Swiss. They also learned that further down the lake the banks were also in Italy although the Swiss pleasure steamers studiously kept to their own side of the frontier.

James wondered what it must have been like in his father's time when other escaping airmen of the USAF and their allies tried to get over the border. Did the guards on the Swiss side turn a blind eye to anyone trying to get through or did they apply a strict neutrality and prevent those brave lads reaching their freedom? By all accounts that James had heard from his father in the past it must have been quite an experience.

Deciding that their wives would probably still not be ready to move on in view of the number of shops that there were in the town the two men found a small café and settled down to a beer. There were none of the heavy dark beers they had seen in English pubs, rather they were offered the local light lager brew, and it was cold! Good for the Swiss!

At last the ladies appeared. Helen had purchased a couple of calendars. They had pretty pictures on some pages of the little Swiss wooden houses as well as others of those memorable cows with their even more memorable bells around their thick necks. There was even one month with a Swiss train on it. Meantime when Noah asked Christina what she had been buying in that gaily wrapped small red and white paper parcel with a big red bow, he received a non-committal 'nothing much, just a few bits'. But he knew his wife by now, his adorable new wife, and he had a suspicion that her slight flick of an eyebrow was telling him that she was going to return that adoration later on that evening.

A quick walk back to the car and they were off to Italy. It was quite a fast road and it only took twenty minutes for them to reach the border. The British number plate on the Hertz car and a wave of their American passports and they were through. How funny, it seemed as if the only cars being stopped were Italian ones returning home. Once in Italy the driving of all about them, behind and in front, seemed to change dramatically. Indeed no one seemed to stay behind them for a minute more than they needed to. It was not just the large red Alfa Romeos and Ferraris that overtook, even the small Fiats were apparently driven by maniacs. They glimpsed a small little yellow car that was being driven by a priest and with a nun in the back. It was as if the devil himself was chasing them and that they had to get to the Vatican before the pursuing monster caught up with them. 'What had those two been up to?' James mused to himself before coming to the conclusion that he must be charitable in his thoughts and assume that there was some poor soul badly in need of ministrations.

The strong Italian sun seemed to move all around them as they twisted and turned. There were still plenty of hills to climb and hairpin bends to traverse before at long last they saw ahead a long stretch of water. It was Lake Garda.

CHAPTER XVI

Italy 2006

The long lake, long by European standards but of course not by American, seemed to run from the north to the south and the further down it went the more gentle became the mountains on either side. Towards the far end it divided into two parts with a tiny strip of land separating it into two parts. Their destination, Desenzano, was at the far end of the right-hand stretch of the lake. The town was backed by a low ridge of gentle hills behind it. They stopped at a viewpoint and looked down the lake. Somewhere over the other side had been the scene of that terrible fight by the Italian partisans against the German army and in which Theo had played his part whilst futilely trying to escape to Switzerland.

Helen could read her husband's thoughts and gently slid her fingers so that they intermingled with his. He returned the embrace with a soft squeeze that said volumes between husband and wife. If only Theo could have been with them that day. He would have realised that all that terrible fighting, the ghastly deaths of his new-found friends, and even his later incarceration in a prisoner-of-war camp in Germany had been worthwhile, for peace had descended on that beautiful scene. Now there was freedom there; Americans, Brits, and all the peoples of Europe, including their former German enemies, were able to take their holidays in Europe without fear. They could cross boundaries almost without being aware of them and all could talk openly to ex-ally and ex-foe alike without fear of interrogation or imprisonment for their ideas. For sure it had all been worthwhile, but those heroes who managed to bring it about by sacrificing their lives should never be forgotten.

However it was time to move on and get to their hotel before the early dark evening arrived. In another forty minutes they were off the fast main roads and negotiating the outskirts of Desenzano looking for their hotel.

'There it is, the "Garda Supremo",' suddenly shouted Christina and they slowed down and entered the gates of a large old house with its name on the wall outside. It was a beautiful old building to which had been added a modern but tastefully-designed block of new rooms. There was ample room to park and a fine swimming pool in the front garden. At the rear the grounds sloped gently down to the edge of the lake surrounded as they were by evergreen bushes and areas for sunbathing. Stepping out of the car they paused and stood looking out over the lake to the northern distant Alps beyond, whence they had just come.

'What a beautiful place,' said Helen as she picked up her lovely new Swiss red leather shoulder bag, which she had bought only that morning in Lugano, and prepared to go up the steps into the hotel.

They dined in the hotel that evening, the youngsters realising that it had been a long and tiring day for Christina's parents-in-law. After James and Helen moved into the hotel lounge for a quiet drink the youngsters announced they would take a short walk into the town so as to get their bearings for the next day. Nine-thirty in the evening was not the time to go to bed in Desenzano. Rather it was the time for the traditional "Passeggiata" when half the town's population decided to stroll along the lakeside – the "Lungolaga" as it was known – or to sit in one of the little cafés with a local beer or glass of wine and watch everyone else walking up and down.

By the little pier were tied up three lakeside steamers awaiting the next morning's customers. One was a paddle steamer, not just any paddle steamer with its white superstructure and awning to protect the tourists from the following day's sun, but a paddle steamer with a history. Her name, "Italia", was painted in black on her side. She had been used as a German hospital-ship on the lake during the war and doubtless Theo would from his hideaway up in the hills have espied her plying to and fro at the time. In 1945 she had been bombed and sunk off the little town of Sirmione. But now she was back once more, and in happier times. She was ready to take the next day's tourists for an excursion around Lake Garda. Tied up near the Italia were two more modern motor vessels awaiting the call of duty once all the visitors were up and about the following day.

The two young folk, for still being in their early thirties such they still felt about each other, were both on their second marriages due to that terrible day in Manhattan five years ago, yet now they had a common bond in a son of their own together. Noah glanced discreetly at his beautiful wife sitting there in the warm Italian evening air and watching the gentle waves of the lake lap lapping the stone quayside. She was happy and she was relaxed. For a moment his mind flicked back to Rachel, her beautiful black breasts and long, long legs. Five years ago tonight she had told him she was pregnant with their first child but then two days later she and their whole future together had disappeared in a cloud of dust and an orgy of fire due to those damned terrorists. Why had they done it? Did they not have families of their own? Had it not been their first duty to look after their own wives and children rather than to steal the happiness of others by their dastardly acts of terrorism?

In many ways – so sad ways and yet so inevitable ways – the world had moved on and here he was with Christina and in the very town where her grandfather and others had been hunted by the Gestapo. Over there amongst the rocks and trees of that hillside up the lake the old man had fought for his life – and for the very peace and tranquillity that tonight they, Noah and Christina, could enjoy together.

After all their travelling the four of them had decided that the next day would be a quiet day and that they would leave the car at the hotel and go for a sail on the lake. A leisurely breakfast after an early dip in the pool and the four of them walked down to the quayside to buy their tickets.

The last time James had been in Italy, on a business trip to give a lecture at Bologna University, he had had to pay for everything in Italian lire but now most of Europe was using the same currency. It was called the "Euro". At least it meant they did not have to keep changing the money in their wallets and purses every time they had crossed into another country. Much more sensible, it was rather like using the same US dollar all over at home and not having to change the bills every time they crossed from Connecticut to New York State or from New Jersey to Pennsylvania. Only England and a handful of others had stuck to their traditional money.

But the Brits were like that, they seemed to have a built-in resistance to change. Maybe if they had been a bit more flexible in their ideas over two hundred years ago the Boston

Tea Party would never have taken place and the US might still have had the British Queen. But it was hard to imagine that.

The "Italia" was still tied up at the jetty as they bought their tickets and then went on board. They quickly found seats under the awning on the top deck and had no sooner done so than with a few shouts from the crew the ropes were loosened, the big side paddles started to churn the waters in the small harbour and she was off. For twenty or so minutes the little steamer headed north-easterly up the lake to the long spur of land they had seen the previous day and which seemed to split the lower part of the lake into two. Noah had his camera at the ready, the one Christina had given him as a present just before they left home. Gradually the "Italia" approached a lakeside town dominated by a castle which had a flag flying from its tower. This was Sirmione, the same Sirmione that the same "Italia" had been heading for in 1945 when, while helping with German and Italian wounded, she had been sunk by Allied bombers. Now she was carrying tourists from all over the globe. Near them were a German family, probably oblivious of the experiences of their fellow countrymen all those years ago, and beyond the Germans were a couple of young Japanese. By the looks of it they were on their honeymoon judging by the exchanges that they kept giving to each other.

Arriving at Sirmione the four of them got off, and what a good job they did, for there was a long line-up of folk waiting to go further up the lake that morning. Helen guessed the ship might have been a bit overcrowded for comfort. Either side of the jetty where they had disembarked were a number of hotels with their own pools and sunbathing patios but straight ahead was what seemed to be a little square with shops and cafes all around. There were tourists everywhere, more per square inch than in Times Square back home on a Saturday evening. It was a bit like the outside of the UN building in Manhattan, so many different languages were being spoken.

At the far end of the square was a large shop counter selling ice cream. Every colour and every flavour you could imagine was on display. Christina chose a green pistachio one whilst Helen opted for a blueberry. Both men went for the more conventional strawberry and vanilla versions. Holding the cones and licking their chosen flavours they meandered through the tiny streets and headed for the castle. The tall grey stone building was surrounded by water and nearby was a bridge over the moat. Alongside the bridge was a street vendor's stall and which was selling the largest yellow lemons that Christina or the others had ever seen. Beyond was a tree-lined park at the edge of which a policewoman kept turning away almost any traffic that tried to enter the little streets of the town. Only vehicles that were either small vans, or cars belonging to hotel residents, were permitted to enter and then only at a snail's pace to weave in between the tourists.

They traced their steps back into the square and then beyond. They had been told that it was about a ten minute walk to some old Roman remains at the top end of the little isthmus that divided the two parts of the lake. Those ten minutes seemed to take almost twice that time for the burning hot sun played on their heads, arms and legs although mercifully all of them had taken the precaution to wear sun-hats of differing designs. Finally they arrived at the end of the promontory to find a fantastic display of ancient walls and buildings that had once been used to guard the southern end of the lake from invaders who had come from the other side of the far off Alps which they could see in the distance.

Once they had walked round the old walls and Noah had taken his fill of photographs they returned to the town centre to find a small restaurant where they could eat some lunch accompanied by a bottle of "Bardolino". This was apparently the local red wine and was named after another lakeside town further up. Mid-afternoon found them sailing back to Desenzano on a much smaller and more modern motor launch than the old "Italia". It was a relief to sit on the upper open deck and find the breeze playing on their faces and arms after the burning sun when in Sirmione.

On the Wednesday after their arrival, breakfast was taken early by the pool. Few other guests had appeared downstairs as the two couples worked their way through a breakfast of cereals, fruit juices, bread rolls and coffee. The friendly head waiter, anxious as always to please, enquired if they were going somewhere special that day.

'We are going to Venice for the day,' replied Helen. 'My husband and I have been before but our daughter-in-law and her husband have never been there.'

'Ah, Venezia, bello, bello,' he replied. 'It is so easy to go from here for the day. You take the train? There are many beautiful things to see. Every gentleman must take his lady to Venezia.' The head waiter turned to Noah and gave him a big wink.

It was not long before their taxi arrived to take them up to the stazione above the town. The rail tickets were ridiculously cheap by US standards and the long train with seventeen carriages was quite full as they clambered into their First Class seats. Around them were many morning commuters making the two hour journey towards Venice. Some were reading the newspapers whilst the younger executives more frequently were heads down into their laptops and with wires protruding from their ears. Whilst the Italians amongst the passengers seemed to be studying or working away quietly, the silence would not infrequently be broken by a high-pitched voice from some tourist or other; for a significant number of the seats were taken up by international travellers making the same pilgrimage to Venice as themselves. Many were evidently going to spend a few days in the city as pull-along valises and large bags were to be seen in every available spare place both above heads on racks and in the centre aisle. The train made three or four stops at other towns on the way and through the windows Christina could see all the platforms seemed crowded. Especially noticeable were the number of teenage students who each appeared to be attending colleges in any other town than their own.

The first station at which they had stopped was Verona. On the adjacent platform was a green and white train. Like many others they had seen on the European mainland, the coaches carried little metal plates on the outside showing passengers the stations of their route. This one evidently had started in Munchen ('Munich, in Germany,' explained James) and was going via Verona to 'Roma' – Rome.

'I wonder how many hours that takes?' mused Helen. 'It must be fascinating to travel by train through different countries and scenery, all without moving from your seat.'

There was so much to see out of the window, and so many fellow travellers to observe, that it was no time before they noticed that there was water on both sides of the train. On the left side the water stretched away into the distance. But it could not be deep because it was covered with small wooden posts that seemed to form triangles that indicated passage-ways of deeper water channels. On the other side of the train was an expressway with automobiles and busses racing in both directions and beyond which was more water with distant shipyards.

'We are on a causeway and nearly there now,' announced James as he reached up to put on his straw hat that would protect him from the blazing Venetian sun outside.

With a screeching of metal upon metal as the brakes were applied, the engine brought all seventeen coaches of the long train from Milan to a gentle halt. As they stepped down onto the platform Christina noticed crews of cleaners were already at work washing the windows of the new arrival with water from a little truck whilst others were starting to go through the coaches removing old newspapers and giving each table a quick wipe-over before the train filled up again for the return journey.

But, oh my! How impressive could you be for a railway station? As they walked through the station lobby and out the far side they found themselves at the top of a flight of wide steps with a view of the Grand Canal in front of them. Everywhere there were people, and everywhere there were little boats of all shapes and sizes. Sleek, and doubtless very fast, motor boats that looked as if they had just delivered some film star to her hotel, slower ponderous barge-shaped vessels piled high with boxes and crates for delivery to some warehouse or other, and weaving in between in those always-turbulent waters a number of low-lying faded-cream coloured passenger vessels. They were the famous water buses of Venice – the 'vaporetti'.

'Let's get on one of those, it looks like fun,' said Christina, her eyes almost bursting with excitement.

'We'll get day-tickets, then we can go all round on them,' said her father-in-law, smiling over at Helen who was enjoying not just the scenery but also the pleasure of seeing her daughter-in-law so happy.

'My guide book says the Number One to Saint Mark's Square,' responded Noah as they bought their tickets at the kiosk and walked onto the floating pontoon. A couple of minutes later the No. 1 arrived and half of Venice seemed to try and get on to the little vessel, to join the other half already on board! Although squashed in between other tourists and local Venetians going about their daily business, it was truly fun as the vessel set off along the Grand Canal.

'Look, we are going under a bridge,' squealed Christina.

'That is the world-famous Rialto Bridge,' explained James as they passed beneath an old stone structure with steep sides over which crowds of visitors to the city were leaning with their cameras photographing the boats passing below. On one side were more little floating boat-stations where the vaporetti would take turns at pulling in to deliver and collect more travellers whilst on the other side the quay was covered with restaurants and diners having their morning cappuccinos.

As they progressed further down the canal the buildings on both sides seem to keep becoming more and more impressive. Virtually all seemed to be hundreds of years old. Painted in different colours and with the wall surfaces often peeling away, the buildings each had not only windows overlooking the canal but large front doors on a step just above the water level. Each entrance was marked by two large white dome-capped poles diagonally painted with blue or red stripes and which projected out from the canal bottom. Evidently you walked out of your front door into your own motor boat or perhaps a waiting water-taxi. The scene was one of a real highway of little boats of all sorts, but perhaps the most impressive of all were the long sleek gondolas. Each boasted a high prow at both ends and they seemed to be propelled by a single oarsman wearing a flat straw hat.

'Look at that one. He has a tee shirt like mine,' sang out Christina.

'Ah, but his has red and white stripes whilst you look gorgeous in your blue and white one,' replied her husband as he took the opportunity to photograph his lovely wife against a background of a passing red-stucco building adorned with a banner proclaiming the merits of the museum inside its walls.

'San Marco, San Marco,' called out the rasping voice of the crew member as the little vaporetto nudged and bumped itself against the floating jetty.

Standing in St Mark's Square in Venice for the first time in her life was something Christina would never forget. On three sides of the square the buildings had colonnades that protected those who wished to be in the shade from the fierce overhead sun while enabling them to see all around. At the head of the square was the "Duomo", the Cathedral, with a long line-up of tourists waiting to have the opportunity to go inside, whilst part-way down the open square was the tall orange brick tower of the Campanile. A number of cafés seemed to occupy parts of two of the square's sides and each had its own orchestra playing popular tunes. Yet the square was so large that if you sat with your espresso at one set of tables enjoying the music you could not hear the melodies of the other on the far side.

'This is on me, please,' said Christina as all four drew up chairs and ordered their coffees from the white-jacketed waiter who seemed to appear from nowhere as soon as they sat down. A latte for Helen, an espresso for each of the two husbands and she herself asked for a cappuccino.

The music was enchanting, the sun was beating down out of the azure Venetian sky and the world seemed to be at their feet. Perhaps for the first time since her world had been torn apart five years before Christina felt really at peace. She closed her eyes and as she did so the violinist and the cellist ever so gently seemed to float into that haunting tune she had heard only a few days before in Lugano. "Volare" wafted through the warm calm air around her. It was almost as if she never wanted to open her eyes again but rather to keep that moment into oblivion, to float upwards, up beyond the very top spire of the Campanile tower and into the heavens. Maybe Robert was up there amongst the white angels reaching down with arms outstretched to welcome her.

She was woken out of her reverie with a clap of Noah's hands. A pigeon, one of the thousands of pigeons that seemed to have made St Mark's Square their home, had landed on the table and was starting to peck at the small biscuit beside her coffee cup.

'Be off with you, whoosh!' Noah was clapping his hands to scare the grey bird away. It flapped its wings and disappeared off into a cloud of fellow companions who were wheeling and diving around looking for some other bits of broken biscuit or nuts that a tourist might have bought from one of the vendors with barrows, and whose lives seemed to exist as suppliers of corn and nuts for the winged occupants of the square.

When the music from the little orchestra came to a brief halt the metal chairs were pushed back and all four Americans set off to explore once more. At one side of the cathedral was a narrow lane that led off into a myriad of small squares and equally tiny streets. All along and at every step there appeared to be yet another small shop. Many were offering souvenirs of the city whilst some had windows full of masks. Noah's guide book had explained that these masks were traditionally worn at big dances or "balls" by Venetian Society during the weeks of the Carnival before the start of Lent. They were supposed to disguise the wearer during a period when society abandoned the strict moral codes of the rest of the year and laxity and self-indulgence appeared to be accepted by all.

All the tiny lanes seemed to be so crowded, with folk often having to inch past each other, until emerging from between two buildings they came upon a small canal. It was equally narrow and crowed with gondolas carrying their international human cargoes from so many nations. Most of the gondoliers had those same sort of striped jerseys and from one little vessel came the melodious wafting of an accordion. The scene reminded Noah of traffic back in Manhattan, except whereas on Lexington or Third Avenue the yellow taxis seemed to drive fast, despite their numbers, here in Venice the progress was much slower and sedate. Some rush-hour!

Finally with their Venice day over and as the Milan-bound train taking them back to their hotel in Desenzano rumbled across the Causeway out of the city, Christina settled back into her comfortable soft blue seat and closed her eyes once more. It had been a wonderful day and how lucky they were to be staying in that hotel from which they could go for day excursions to so many fantastic places. And all because just over sixty years ago her Robert's grandfather had come to Italy on a bombing mission and then been shot down by a supposedly-neutral Swiss unlucky hit. What would the next sixty years bring?

Answer came there none, for as the seventeen carriages hauled by that electric locomotive passed through Padua, Vicenza and once more Verona, Christina was in her own very private world.

Another day the two couples decided to each go their different ways. Whilst James and Helen went on another lake trip going further up that long stretch of water so that they could see more of the small lakeside towns at which the steamer called, Noah and Christina decided to visit Verona, the nearest large city part-way to Venice.

It was fun travelling by the local bus service so as to absorb the Italian atmosphere. The blue bus had stopped near their hotel and was already part-full as they set off on the hour's trip. Noah had read up his guide-book the previous evening whilst Christina had been taking a long shower. At first the bus would skirt the southern end of the lake and would then cross the old boundary where at one time Italy and the Austrian Empire had met. Sure enough even to this day by the roadside was a yellow building with the name 'Ristorante Dogana' – 'border restaurant' – clearly showing. But now it was all Italy and they stopped to let down some passengers at a lakeside town called Peschiara. At one time the town been a major military base for the Austrians and they could see a large fortress building together with its old and very large once-military barracks. How things had changed – and for the better of course. Now with one currency and almost invisible borders the world seemed a safer place.

Finally the bus arrived at the terminus next to the railway station at Verona. Beyond it stood a large stone arch that at some time had been part of the old city walls but the one-time Roman centurions who had guarded this entrance to the city had now given way to a continual wave of fast traffic that surged into the town centre. Christina and Noah walked hand in hand through the arch and towards the city. Verona appeared to be a very prosperous place. Many of the buildings were offices in substantial grey stone structures but then… they could only gasp. They had entered a large square at one corner of which was a high circular building, some of it formed by stone arches. This was the ancient Roman Forum that had been there for nearly two thousand years. The guide book had warned them to expect it but its proportions seemed to reach through the centuries, from the days of gladiators fighting each other to the death and Christians being thrown to the lions to see if their god could save them, right down to modern times when concerts were performed late at night featuring some of Italy's greatest operas. They needed a coffee so as to gather their thoughts and for half an hour the two of them scarcely spoke as their individual imaginations took them through two thousand years of history. Gee these Europeans did have something to shout about!

But there was much more to see in Verona and then there was still the long bus journey back. The guidebook had said a

The beautiful old harbour at Desenzano, Lake Garda.

Paddle steamer 'Italia'
Built 1909. Sunk off Sirmione by Allied bombers whilst acting as a hospital ship, January 1945.
Returned to service in 1952 and still carrying tourists in 2014!

Lemon stall near the entrance to Sirmione Castle, Lake Garda.

Verona's 2000-year-old amphitheatre, still used for operas in the 21ˢᵗ century.

Traffic congestion, Venice-style!

Gondola factory and repair yard, Venice.
All photos in this section by Peter Pennington.

"must" was to visit the balcony where Juliet had been serenaded by her own true Romeo. They set off through some of the narrow streets that were lined with really expensive shops until they found their way beneath a little arch and there at the end was the scene of Shakespeare's famous love scene. Indeed it was perhaps the most famous love story ever. The little area below the high-up balcony was crowded with tourists – another gathering of the United Nations – and on some of the walls young lovers had scribbled their names. Unfortunately Juliet was out that morning; perhaps she was spending her money in some of those fabulous shops, but the atmosphere was great and Christina laid her head on Noah's shoulder and squeezed his hand tightly. They would have their own love scene back at the hotel later that night. She was determined on that.

It was a beautiful warm evening as back in the hotel and after dinner the four of them sat at a small table overlooking the floodlit swimming pool. It was so peaceful and quiet. No one was allowed to go swimming after night-fall so they could talk quietly and see the reflection of the hotel lights bouncing back from the blue waters that seemed to radiate peace to all around. A couple of other tables were occupied by different groups including a party of four Englishmen who were staying at the hotel whilst on a golfing holiday.

At another table an elderly Italian husband and his wife were just sitting almost without exchanging words with each other. That situation was a challenge to any American and Helen could not resist smiling at the old lady and greeting her with 'Buona sera signora'. It was about the limit of Helen's Italian but it served its purpose.

'Ah, good evening, you are inglese, excuse me, English?' came the response.

They had seen the old dears arrive late that afternoon and they were obviously regulars as the signora was greeted with kisses on both cheeks by the head waiter when they had come into dinner.

'American actually,' Helen replied. 'We are from New England.'

'Si, si, American. I understand. You are here on holiday then?'

Helen half-swivelled her chair to face the old lady.

'Yes, we have been to Switzerland and before that to England. This is my husband, James and our daughter-in-law and her husband,' she said with a gesture to each of them in turn.

All this time the old man remained quiet and Helen was not sure whether he was understanding the conversation or not.

'So why you come here and not to Firenze or Roma?' came the enquiry.

'My husband's father was here many years ago,' Helen replied. 'He was here during the war'. At this James shot a warning glance at his wife. She could be treading in dangerous waters. The old folk were ancient enough that they may have been involved in those days; they might even have supported Mussolini and the Germans. But Helen ignored her husband's looks and continued.

'Actually he was in those hills over there,' she gesticulated across to the other side of the lake.

The old man shifted his legs. James was pretty sure he understood what was being said.

'Perche? Why? When was he there?' the old lady seemed to say in a most casual way.

'Nineteen forty-three,' Helen replied, but James intervened.

'Actually 1944, my dear.'

'Mille nova cento quaranta quarto,' the old lady repeated in Italian turning to her husband.

'Si, capito,' he replied, then turning to face James, 'Con i partigiani?' he asked. 'Excuse, with the partigiani?'

'Why yes, actually,' James responded and he felt he was going a little pale in the face and his lips were starting to get dry. 'He was escaping from the Germans and trying to get to Switzerland. But he was captured and sent to a prisoner-of-war camp after helping the partisans attack an enemy convoy.'

The old man seemed to draw a deep breath.

'Si, it was, how you say, 'a big fight'. I was there. We had due americani with us. I do not remember their names but they were our good friends. We lost many friends that day. Ronaldo, Lupo and my fratello, my brother, Franco... it was a sad day but we stopped that convoy.'

James could scarcely believe his ears. Here, sitting at the pool-side, was one of those very men who had helped his father, Theo, and many of whose friends had given up their lives on that terrible day. Just over there in those hills that were now disappearing in the darkness as the fading sun set behind them.

'May I buy you a drink, sir?' asked James. The old boy glanced up at his wife.

'Perhaps a little one for him,' she replied on her husband's behalf. 'His medico says he must not have too much.'

James beckoned over the waiter who soon returned with a small grappa. He knew what his guest liked.

'Salute' came from the next table as the old war hero raised his glass to James and Helen. Then came the silence. James was itching to start plying his new friend with a dozen, no not a dozen a hundred, questions but he realised the old chap had had become lost in the past. His wife noticed that James was intrigued but she gently motioned with her hand in a way that only one woman can to another. Helen got the message and reaching over the table to James she in turn squeezed his. She knew he was trembling a little but he got the message and just sat without saying a word.

Maybe it was the grappa, maybe it was just that the old man felt that perhaps now, at long last and to a new generation, he should do his duty by history and tell these young Americans a little of those days.

It was now more than sixty years since the death of his brother Franco and the others. One day historians would write of those times, but they would not have been there. They would not have known the true feelings of lying in the grass amongst the bushes in the early-morning dew, and with a horrible feeling in the stomach of not knowing whether, when the last rays of the evening sun glowed and vanished from the waters of Lake Garda, one would still be alive.

The old man himself was now in his mid-eighties and he had lived to see the end of that war and the defeat of fascism. He had even seen the end of the House of Savoy and the Italian monarchy followed by the birth instead of a new republic. And now his beloved Italy was being merged by the politicians in Rome into a new European Union so that old enemies were supposed to be their new and everlasting friends. Was that what Franco and the others had died for? They had sacrificed everything, but he had survived.

Now perhaps was his last chance to tell what had really happened. His wife would help him. She knew his story and could speak a little inglese.

The old man closed his eyes and his mind travelled back more than six decades. He took a deep breath...

It was a funny war, funny not in the way that it made people laugh, rather it made so many cry, but it had been so different to the First War, "La Prima Guerra", about which he and Franco had heard so much from their father.

The family had always lived in Desenzano. His father, and his father before him, had been butchers. They had had a shop in a little side-street just off the Piazza Moretti in the centre of the town. His father had worked hard in that shop and the only times he could remember his father leaving the premises was on a Tuesday morning when he always set up a stall in the market place with the hope that he would sell a little more meat that day, and a few extra lire would tinkle into the cash box he kept under the shop counter.

In those days the whole area had something of a "Wild West" feeling. A bit like those pictures he had seen of America in the cinema in the nearby town of Brescia. After all Italy had only started to become one single country in the 1860s after defeating the Austrians, who had traditionally occupied the eastern shores of the lake. Indeed Vienna had still controlled the northern end of the lake until 1922, just before Franco had been born.

Many of the big battles for Italian Independence had been fought very close to Desenzano. Perhaps the most famous of all had been that at nearby Solferino. It was the terrible bloody scenes there that had given rise to the birth of the Red Cross. One of his grandfathers had died at Solferino – and then two generations and eighty years later Franco had done the same. All for Italy – and freedom.

Maybe without the courage of his grandfather the border with Austria would still be 10 kilometres from where they were all sitting that evening; and maybe the big fortress at Peschiera only 15 kilometres away at the south-east corner of the lake would still have an Austrian garrison. Even maybe there would still be an Austrian naval base at Lazise with its patrol boats glaring across the lake from the Veneto side at Desenzano and Italian Lombardy?

These young tourists needed to know these things if they were to understand his family history, because it seemed now that it was also part of their family history as well.

He had heard from his father that in those days Desenzano was a bustling port. The railway had constructed a special track down to the quayside so that it could carry away the textiles, the fish, the products from the paper-mills and even the lemons from the town of Limone: all of which were on the Italian side of the lake, and which could not reach their customers and markets in other countries through Austria because of high tariffs. All these products came down to Desenzano in a fleet of little sailing boats and small steamers. There the bales of paper, the rolls of textiles, the boxes of fish and the crates of lemons were loaded onto the trains and the big black smoky engines would trundle past the very hotel where they were now all sitting, up to the main line taking the products of Gardaside off to Milano, to Firenze and perhaps even to far-off places like England and America.

After the end of that First World War the Austrians had left the lake and had retired to the other side of the Alps. They had fought hard to keep their territory on the sunny southern slopes and those terrible winters of 1916-17 and 1917-18 had witnessed many brave acts, by both sides, high up in the alpine snows. Men had fought and died in deep snow drifts on the front line. They had needed to use their ice axes to dig holes in the snow and from where they could better both sleep and fight. Often supplies, everything from guns and ammunition to food and clothing, had been hauled up the snow-covered mountain slopes and over deep crevices using ropes that swung in the freezing wind and provided a target for their enemies. If the ropes were destroyed, the lifeline for the soldiers had gone. When that happened they fought until the last bullet and shell but then many just faded away as the bitter winds enveloped them and finally the fresh snow covered them where they lay. Even now climbers still sometimes found the bodies of those brave Italian alpini and their Austrian counterparts.

Only some twenty years later Italy was again at war. Her fascist prime minster, Benito Mussolini, had made friends with the Nazi government in Germany and during those twenty years between the two conflicts his, and Franco's, Italy had become a one-party state ruled from Rome. Little by little as the fascists had extended their influence and control in the 1920s and '30s all other political parties had disappeared. To some Italians the methods had been acceptable. Society became used to a greater discipline. Some people had even benefited – but you had to be on the right side to see that. Others simply had put their heads down and got on with trying to live as normal a life as possible. It was said in praise of the new system that now at long last 'the trains ran on time'. But at what cost? Year by year in those days the foreign tourists had started to go elsewhere; not because they were personally in danger but because the atmosphere was not conducive to a relaxed happy holiday for those Americans, British and others who could afford to travel. At least the tourists could go elsewhere and finally travel home to their own countries. But for the ordinary Italians you did not talk about these things. You followed the rules, but in your heart of hearts... and the fascists could not get there!

Just as sometimes one would look up to the northern end of the lake and see dark clouds gathering over the distant Alps so it seemed to many the dark clouds of war were beginning to gather once more.

Then the war finally arrived. First England and France had declared war on Germany after the invasion of Poland by Hitler's forces and then in 1940 the government in Rome decided to invade southern France. Governments in Rome had never forgotten that France had acquired Savoy in their country's north-west corner and they had lost a large piece of territory including towns such as Nice on the Mediterranean coast. Perhaps now was an opportunity to get them back?

But all that seemed a long way away from wartime Desenzano and the other Garda lakeside towns. The local hotels were still full of tourists but the British, the Americans, the Dutch and others had been replaced by those from Saxony and Bavaria in Germany. In the cafés of the town Italian girls fraternised with German soldiers who had come to "help" the Italians. At night, on the high railway viaduct at the edge of the town, could be heard the rumble of frequent freight trains bringing ammunition, tanks and other supplies of war from over the Brenner Pass and German and Austrian factories beyond. On the lake itself the steamers still plied for those "new" tourists and the meat supplies for his father were still flowing almost normally. But late at night if one wandered down in the darkened streets to the port area – and kept clear of the ever-patrolling sentries – one could stand against an unlit lamp-post, smoke a cigarette and from up above it was possible to hear the distinctive drone of big aeroplanes. American planes, and at night especially British planes, who had been dropping bombs on the industrial cities of Milan, Turin, Parma and elsewhere.

If secretly in your heart of hearts you welcomed the message brought by those planes, and hoped that one day the fascists would disappear from the Italian peninsula, as had the Huns and the Byzantines many centuries before, you kept those feelings to yourself.

Suddenly one day things started to change. First Sicily and then the south of the Italian peninsula had been invaded and liberated by the Allies. In Desenzano German troops swarmed everywhere and security was tightened up. Incredibly the news came that the King had dismissed Mussolini and the new government in Rome had decided to change sides.

Marshal Bagdolio, who had once been Mussolini's Commander-in-Chief, was now the new Prime Minister of an anti-Mussolini government.

During that dreadful winter of 1943-44 the two sides faced each other across the "leg" of Italy. The Apennine ridge of mountains down the spine of the country became one big mud-bath and it was only very, very slowly that Allied armies began to creep up that long leg that was their beloved country.

The impact on Desenzano was there to be seen if one looked. The girls – at least the good girls – no longer met their German corporals or young lieutenant friends at a café. Patrols were stepped up and searches made suddenly in both homes and businesses. Without a word being said in public it was known that some young men were disappearing from the towns and villages. Little groups of partisans were being formed; and on dark nights, in isolated areas, parachutes with containers of arms and ammunition were being dropped by Allied aircraft to bolster both the fighting power and the morale of these brave young men. The age of the Partigiani had come to Lake Garda. They were prepared to fight and give their lives for the cause of freedom.

But so had Mussolini come to Lake Garda. The ex-Prime Minister set up a new government on the lake. The small town of Salo, less than 20 kilometres away on the left hand side of the lake from Desenzano, became the new seat of power for what was remaining, and it was a big amount then still under the control of fascist Italy. Although a small lakeside town, Salo was adjacent to Gardone, which until only five years before had been the long-term residence of Italy's famous poet d'Annunzio – a strong supporter of Mussolini.

With its fine buildings and large church, Salo became the recognised seat of a real national administration. The governments of Germany's (and Mussolini's) friends all her neck to set off her fawn-coloured blouse and skirt. He was thick-set, almost a square head and with just a glimmering of a moustache that hinted of perhaps a sandy head of hair in the past. They were from a different world to the two younger Americans and yet they had all been touched in the past by the fingers of fate. Could this old man really have once held a lethal machine gun of some sorts and mowed down German troops sitting in a truck? Could he have thrown grenades at another human being who had themselves perhaps been a husband or a father? Man could be so unkind to man.

'Come on my honey, time for bed! We have had a long day in Verona,' said Noah as he softly eased Christina to her feet and guided her by the elbow to the lobby lift.

Later on in the quiet of their lovely room, and after the last empty wine bottles had been noisily tipped into the garbage bins somewhere near the kitchens down below, and peace and quiet had enveloped all about them, Noah murmured into his beautiful companion's ear.

'You know my sweet, we have seen history today. We have seen where Christians were put into the area to be torn apart for Roman entertainment and we have met a man who was prepared two thousand years later to sacrifice his life to save that same Christianity.'

'I know,' she replied as she gently ran her fingers over Noah's chest. 'We have much to be thankful for.' She snuggled closer to him.

Tomorrow was September 11th. Five years tomorrow morning she had woken early and had made love with Robert. She knew from what Noah had once told her that the same had happened to him and Rachel early that fateful morning. A tear trickled down her cheek and made a tiny pool on Noah's chest. He knew why and as their fingers clasped together Christina and Noah slipped into oblivion for a few blessed hours.

Tomorrow was tomorrow and they had both to leave the past, albeit a precious past, behind them. They slept, the hotel slept and somewhere in another bedroom, on another floor, an elderly Italian couple found the peace for which he had fought so bravely, so very bravely, all those years ago. Buona notte!

There were many all over the world who finally went to sleep that night but only after tears had rolled down their cheeks.

Tomorrow was Monday. The eleventh of September. "9/11".